THE LUCY WILSON MYSTERIES

CURSE OF THE MIRROR CLOWNS

CHRIS LYNCH

CANDY JAR BOOKS · CARDIFF
2018

Range Editor: Shaun Russell
Cover: Steve Beckett
Editorial: Will Rees, Lauren Thomas & Keren Williams
Continuity Editor: Andy Frankham-Allen
Licensed by Hannah Haisman

Printed and bound in the UK by
4edge, 22 Eldon Way, Hockley, Essex, SS5 4AD

ISBN: 978-1-912535-10-1

Published by
Candy Jar Books
Mackintosh House
136 Newport Road, Cardiff, CF24 1DJ
www.candyjarbooks.co.uk

For Emily, William, and Daniel

IN SPACE THERE ARE MONSTERS

In the deepest, darkest reaches of space, there are monsters.

Out there, in the inky black, past the furthest stars, they bare their teeth and they sharpen their claws. On barren worlds they charge their bombs and load their guns. They fuel their ships and they plot and plan, plot and plan to one day steal away this Earth of ours.

Oh yes, out there in space, there are monsters.

But not just out there.

Because if you were a clever monster, if you were a monster that had really thought about what it would take to dominate this Earth, you wouldn't arrive from the sky in a ship, announcing your intentions. You wouldn't drop bombs and you wouldn't fire guns.

You would come quietly. You would take your time. You would worm your way in, become a part of the world. You would be ordinary. You would be safe. People would recognise you. We would know your name.

You would be... boring. Very old and very boring. Until one day you decided that it was time to strike...

Yes, if you wanted to steal a planet, that is most assuredly the way you would do it.

— CHAPTER ONE —

SWIMMING POOL RULES

Lucy ran down the main corridor of the school, the creature lumbering after her. Skidding to a halt at a corner, she glanced back.

'Stupid craft project!' she shouted, then disappeared around the corner.

The creature shambled on. Toilet rolls, margarine tubs, washing up liquid bottles, tin foil… Every inch of the thing was made from junk, rubbish Lucy had intended to make into a sculpture for art class. Except the junk had had other ideas! Ideas that might have come to something but for the misfortune of coming to life in a school attended by Lucy Wilson.

Lucy popped her head back around the corner. The junk was taking its time.

'Come on!' she shouted, then disappeared again.

The creature sped up, changing its shape as it moved. An arm here, a leg there, it remade itself step by step, gaining speed, gaining on Lucy. It rounded the corner just in time to see her disappear through the door to the school swimming pool.

Lucy raced through the changing rooms. The lights were still on, but school had been closed for a few hours. There was something very strange about being in school after everyone else had gone home. Stranger to Lucy than being chased by a junk monster. There was Lucy, there was school, there was Ogmore-by-Sea... and there were monsters. The most normal thing on the list was the monsters. Lucy knew where she was with monsters.

Reaching the pool, Lucy stopped. She could hear the thing blundering through the changing rooms behind her. She took a step back, then another, until her heels were over the edge of the water. There was nowhere left to go.

The thing burst through the door. It had crashed through the lost property box on its way, adding lost plimsolls, shorts, and t-shirts to its mass. It charged towards Lucy, splitting itself open to form a huge, gaping mouth.

At the last possible moment Lucy dived to one side, landing hard on the tiled floor, feeling water from the pool splash over her as the monster tumbled over the edge. Wincing from the impact, Lucy rolled onto her side and watched as the creature twisted and turned, trying to create a shape that would hold together. Slowly and surely it broke apart, until nothing was left but a layer of junk floating on the surface. There was no scream, no words, no monstrous hand to break the surface of the water and drag Lucy in.

It was simply… over.

Which was just as well, as it was nearly teatime.

As Lucy was getting to her feet, Hobo came clattering through the door of the boys' changing room. He looked at Lucy, then at the pool, then back to Lucy.

'What happened?'

'Art class,' said Lucy with a grin.

'The monster?'

'Water soluble glue. It just couldn't keep itself together.'

Hobo looked at the pool again, watching the junk floating on the surface.

On the water's surface his reflection shimmered alongside Lucy's; the boy who been robbed of his hair and eyebrows by alopecia, and the mixed-race girl with fierce eyes and unmanageable hair who refused, ever, to fit in.

'You could have waited.'

Lucy patted Hobo on the shoulder. 'You'd have slowed me down, Hobo. It's better this way.'

Lucy was through the door to the girls' changing room before Hobo could answer. He would have followed her to the ends of the Earth, but there were some places no boy should ever set foot, and he suspected Lucy knew this too.

Hobo caught up with Lucy just outside the main school building. She was already pushing through a gap in the wire fence.

'You could have waited again,' Hobo panted, struggling to catch his breath.

'I just dumped our class project in the swimming pool,' said Lucy, popping out of the other side of the fence. 'I'm not hanging about to see what happens next!'

'Why not?' asked Hobo. 'What does happen next?'

'If we get caught? Probably quite a bit of detention, I'd imagine.'

Hobo sighed.

'I meant with the monster. The alien. Whatever that thing was.'

'Oh that,' Lucy replied dismissively. 'Yeah, yeah, that's done. Don't worry about it.'

Hobo, fearing the icy grip of the caretaker on his collar, started to push his way through the fence as well.

'Seriously though, Lucy, what was that thing?'

Lucy scuffed her shoe on the ground, pondering.

'The Great Intelligence?' Hobo suggested.

'Maybe,' replied Lucy. 'It seems a bit... crude

though, don't you think? A junk monster?'

Hobo popped out of the fence like a ragged lump of streamers out of a party popper. Lucy dodged out of the way. Having escaped the clutches of a junk monster, she'd have been disappointed to end her adventure crushed by Hobo.

Lucy reached down and helped Hobo to his feet. Side by side, they started to head for home.

'What if,' said Hobo, 'the Great Intelligence left some sort of energy behind, like radiation or something, and that's what animated it?'

Lucy shrugged. 'Yeah, could be. But it's gone now anyway, and I doubt we'll see another.'

'So that's it?' Hobo asked. 'You don't want to investigate?'

'Nah,' said Lucy. 'Thing is, Hobo, when you're like me, these things just happen.'

Hobo had known Lucy long enough to feel a 'Lethbridge-Stewart moment' coming on. He had a nose for it, the way that some animals could sense the impending eruption of a volcano.

'It's all part of being a—'

'Lethbridge-Stewart,' Hobo interrupted, 'I know.'

Lucy shot him a sour look. 'That's right,' she persisted. 'When you're a—'

'Lethbridge-Stewart.'

'Yes,' said Lucy, frustration creeping into her voice. 'It means that monsters just happen. They're like an occupational hazard. It's just that instead of being a policeman or a fireman, I'm a—'

'Lethbridge-Stewart!' spat Hobo.

Lucy threw her hands up in exasperation.

'Will you stop doing that?' she shouted.

'You first,' said Hobo defiantly.

'What do you mean, "Me first"? '

Hobo shook his head. 'The Lethbridge-Stewart thing! For someone who secretly battles aliens, you don't half go on about it! I just wish you'd give it a break every once in a while.'

Lucy shrugged. 'Sorry,' she said sarcastically.

'And it's not just that,' Hobo continued. 'You obviously don't need any help. Not from me, not from anyone. I mean, look at tonight. I thought we were supposed to be a team.'

'You know I didn't mean it like that, Hobo, I just—'

'No, look, so, it's cool being friends and everything but... why don't you just leave me out of all your—'

'Lethbridge-Stewart stuff?' offered Lucy, weakly.

'Yeah,' said Hobo. 'That. For a bit, at least.'

Without realising it, they'd reached the part of their walk home where Hobo turned left and Lucy turned right. They both paused. Each of them wanted the other to take a different route that night, but both of them knew that neither would.

In the end it was Lucy who moved first. Hobo sighed. He was holding her back even now.

'Night then, Hobo,' she said.

'Night.'

Hobo was only a few yards down the road when his resolve cracked. He turned and called after Lucy.

'Hey, Lucy? Did you hear that the circus is coming to town?'

Lucy didn't turn around.

'Lucy?'

'Not my thing, Hobo,' came the eventual reply. 'Kind of not into clowns, to be honest.'

'Oh… OK.'

'Don't let me hold you back though.'

With that, Lucy disappeared around the next corner. Hobo knew that following her now would be even more dangerous than entering the girls' changing room.

— CHAPTER TWO —

THERE, BUT
NOT THERE

Some things have the ability to go unnoticed even when in plain sight. Like the sky – unless you make a special effort to take a really good look, it's just there, one of those things that's right before your eyes but might as well be invisible.

Pete's Punch and Judy box was another one of those things.

Despite being by the sea, Ogmore didn't have what you would call a sea front. Instead it had a car park next to a narrow patch of sand that passed for a beach. If you were lucky, you might find an ice cream van in the car park, although the lure of the richer pickings in Porthcawl Pleasure Beach just up the road often stole it away.

Technically speaking, there was also Pete's Punch and Judy; it was just that nobody ever seemed to notice it.

It was there, but it was also not there.

Pete wasn't actually the owner's name; it was just the name on the booth, but in a place like Ogmore, when people started calling you 'Pete the Punch and Judy Man', it was easier just to go along with it.

Pete was a small man, hunchbacked and hatchet-faced like his Mr Punch puppet. Nobody knew how old he was, and they also didn't know when he arrived in town.

With the sun going down over the slate-grey sea, Pete carefully lifted two wooden cases out of the booth, then secured the booth with a padlock that looked even older and rustier than he was. With a sigh he picked up the cases and began to trudge across the car park.

'Home time, my darlings,' he said to himself. 'Perhaps a bite of macaroni and fish on the way, eh?'

Pete was halfway across the car park when his body stiffened and the boxes went clattering from his hands onto the tarmac. He twitched, as if an electric current were passing through him. His eyes, small and beady, glittered in the quickly fading light as he cast a watchful eye around the car park.

Suddenly, and with an agility that defied his crooked body, he dropped to all fours. Then he began to prowl around like a great hunched dog, sniffing at the ground. For a few moments, he followed invisible trails around the car park. Then he looked up at the darkening sky. Under his breath, with a hiss of anger and hatred, Pete said just one word: 'clown'.

— CHAPTER THREE —
NOT-QUITE-RUINED

Lucy arrived home just in time for her tea. Mum was sitting in front of the television, watching a detective driving a classic car through a country village. Lucy used to hate those shows, back when she'd thought that nothing ever happened outside London.

There was no sign of Dad. He had been called back to London on urgent business two days before. Apart from a cursory text message, there had been no contact with Lucy since. Lucy had been the first to point out – loudly – that it was Dad's work that had dragged them all down to Ogmore-by-Sea in the first place. And now London was calling him back! But just him.

'Is it worth me asking where you've been?' Mum asked from the lounge.

'Just hanging out with Hobo,' replied Lucy, gingerly retrieving her not-quite-totally-ruined tea from the oven. She dumped the piping hot plate onto a tray, grabbed some cutlery, and headed for the stairs.

'You can eat in here with me, you know,' called Mum.

'I know,' replied Lucy, her feet already on the stairs. For all the things she loved about being a Lethbridge-Stewart, she wished that she didn't have to lie to her mum so much. Dad had never explained to Lucy why he'd all but completely broken ties with his side of the family, why he didn't go into the 'family business' in the way that Lucy knew some of her other relatives had. But she could understand his decision a little better now.

For her part, Lucy hoped she was doing her family a favour by keeping them out of her Lethbridge-Stewart business. At least, that was what she told herself when she wanted to avoid an awkward conversation. Any conversation that started with 'So, what did you do in school today?' could categorically *not* end with, 'And so the monster turned out to be only held together by PVA glue, which, as you know, Mum, is water soluble, so I tricked it into falling into the school swimming pool and that was that!'

If Mum did call again, Lucy didn't hear her. She made it to the sanctuary of her bedroom, put the tray on the bed, slumped down onto her bean bag, and suddenly, to her surprise, started to cry. She didn't want to, she really didn't want to, but she did all the same.

Lucy Lethbridge-Stewart-Wilson, scourge of aliens and monsters, totally fearless wonder of south Wales, *cried*.

It wasn't a long cry. It was like that little bit of steam that puffs out of a boiling kettle just before it clicks off. It just needed to come out, that was all. It was probably adrenaline, she told herself. Or maybe she was just tired.

A bit of both, perhaps.

Or maybe what Hobo said had touched a nerve.

Lucy wiped the tears from her cheeks, got up, and looked in the mirror. 'Thanks, Hobo,' she muttered bitterly.

Sitting back down on the bed, she idly picked at the not-quite-totally-ruined tea, not really eating, more waiting for it to congeal into a plate of too-cold-to-bother-with.

Lucy's school friends, Paula and Maya, could always tell when something was wrong because they really cared about her. Like Hobo, they were loyal. But unlike Hobo they knew nothing about the danger she was in or why, and had to be protected. Sometimes that was hard, and she couldn't even message Ayesha in London and hint that life was remotely strange. Only Hobo helped. Until now...

Was this really what it was like, being a Lethbridge-Stewart? Keeping secrets, ruining friendships, being alone? It didn't seem like a big price for the world, but the world wasn't the one paying it. Lucy was. Slumping back on her bed, she stared at the ceiling. She thought about texting Hobo. She thought about getting out her laptop and Skyping her brother. She thought about going downstairs, reheating her already overcooked food and eating it in front of the TV with Mum. But those were all things that normal people did, and Lucy wasn't a normal person. Not anymore.

Things would have been different, could have been different, if she'd stayed in London. For one thing, there were fewer aliens in London. Since coming to Ogmore, Lucy seemed to be knee deep in them. Was it coming to Ogmore that had exposed her? Had it made her stand out?

She supposed it was too late for such questions. Already any chance that Lucy had ever had of fitting in here, of leading a normal life, was gone. She'd always be 'that girl', the one connected to 'that thing that happened'.

Always an outsider.

Lying on her bed, dreading the inevitable sound of Mum climbing the stairs to check on her, Lucy wondered where Lethbridge-Stewarts went when they weren't needed. Because wherever it was, she was there. And it was nowhere at all.

— CHAPTER FOUR —

HARLEQUIN

Pete sat at his usual spot in the window of the fish and chip shop. He came here every Wednesday and always had a small piece of haddock, with chips, and a cup of tea. He would sit down at six, and be gone by six thirty. You could set your watch by it. And your calendar.

But not today. Today was different.

Carol had worked in the fish and chip shop a long time, so long that she could remember Pete's first Wednesday. She had been much younger then, and the fish and chip shop just a summer job.

Since then the summer job had turned into just 'the job', and Carol had gone from being just Carol to 'Fish and Chip Carol'.

But not today. Today was different.

Today, Pete had put a small stack of money on the counter, a pile of crumpled tens and twenties, and asked Carol to cook up two portions of his regular order, and then close up for the night. She'd been reluctant, of course, but the stack of money was far more than the shop would normally take on a Wednesday night, and Pete had suggested that whatever Carol skimmed off the top could be their little secret. He was meeting someone, apparently, and he wanted privacy.

A night off and a purse full of money wasn't to be sniffed at. After all, how much trouble could Punch and Judy Pete and his mystery guest be?

'Here you go, love,' she said, putting two plates of haddock and chips down in front of him. Two cups of tea arrived, quickly followed by the keys to the shop.

'You remember what I explained, about locking up?' she asked.

Pete nodded. 'Lock up. Put keys through letter box. Simple.'

'All right then, love. Well… you have a good night.'

Carol grabbed her purse, stuffed full of as much of the cash as she thought she could get away with, and headed out of the door. Through the greasy window she saw Pete get up, shamble to the door, and turn the latch. He flipped the sign on the door from 'Open' to 'Closed' and turned out the lights. Carol had a sudden pang of worry, seeing the fish and chip shop all in darkness. She thought about waiting, watching to see what happened next, to discover who Pete's mysterious visitor was.

Inside the shop, Pete watched Carol walking away, a shadow just across the street.

With a grunt, he opened up one of his cases, tucked neatly under the bolted down table, and pulled out the stub of a candle. He put it on the table and lit it with a match.

On the other side of the road, glancing back, Carol saw the candlelight.

'So, that's what you're up to, eh?' she said to herself with a smile. 'You romantic old devil.'

Pete watched from inside the shop as Carol waved, smiled, and disappeared off towards home. He kept watch on her until she was gone, then pulled down the shop window blinds. The place was in darkness, save for the light from Pete's candle.

'You can come now,' Pete said to the darkness. 'Come and talk.'

Harlequin always made an entrance. Why walk when you could tumble, or pirouette, or flip, or cartwheel, or combine all of these and more together? Some people thought it was funny, but Pete knew that Harlequin was dangerous – if you ever saw him walking towards you without a twist or a turn or a skip in his step, you were in trouble.

And so Pete waited as Harlequin pranced along the counter, somersaulted down to the floor, and skipped his way to his seat.

Harlequin was wearing a garish suit composed of many different colours. On Earth, Harlequins made their suits from rags and cuttings, with as many fabrics as they could find. But this Harlequin, the real Harlequin, was different. Pete cast his mind back and remembered a boast Harlequin had made about his clothing.

Harlequin's suit wasn't made from scraps of fabric, but from scraps he'd taken from people: a patch of green skin here, a scrap of pale blue there, a piece with fur, another with scales. It was a scrapbook of all the places Harlequin had plied his deadly trade.

Finally Harlequin sat. Pete waited silently. It didn't do to interrupt Harlequin, even if he hadn't started speaking yet.

'This chair is bolted down,' Harlequin said. 'I don't like it.' He looked down at the plate of fish and chips with disgust. 'And is this what they serve here?'

'Is good food.'

'If you say so,' said Harlequin with a sneer. 'Two days ago I dined with the king of the Crystal Cluster.'

Pete nodded his approval, slicing into his fish.

'Sorry,' said Harlequin, laughing, 'I meant I dined *on* the king of the Crystal Cluster. They're crustaceans you know. Very tasty.'

Pete pointed at Harlequin's plate with his fork. 'Is fish. You like fish.'

Harlequin's eyebrows rose up above his domino mask. 'How long have you been here?' he asked pointedly.

'In shop?

'On Earth.'

Pete furrowed his brow.

'Long time.'

Harlequin shook his head, pushing the plate away from him. 'How do you stand it? This place… The smell alone!'

'Is good place,' said Pete. 'Good people.'

'You keep saying that,' said Harlequin, leaning over the table. 'But we both know the truth. You're hiding. You got in your stupid little box and you ran away to hide with the monkeys on their little dirt ball.'

Pete shrugged.

'You know you're not the first to try that?'

Pete sipped his tea. Harlequin was being uncommonly sociable. That didn't bode well – and there were knives on the table.

'Why you come here?' asked Pete.

Harlequin groaned. 'Urgh, you're no fun anymore, you know that? Well if we are dispensing with all the niceties, I'll just come right out with it. I'm here on a job, if you must know.'

'You want help?'

'Moons, no!' said Harlequin, raising his hands in

mock horror. 'I don't want your help! I'm here as a... professional courtesy, one old court turn to another.'

Harlequin got up from the table and idly cartwheeled across the room.

'Pierrot has his eye on a star cluster for Columbine,' he said mid-flip. 'He's given her everything else there is to give in the galaxy, now he's giving her a chunk of the galaxy to go with it.'

'Earth?' asked Pete, nervously.

'Stars, no. Who'd want this dirty old rock? He's planning to give her a star cluster. An actual star cluster! How in all the galaxy do I top that? But I've got a little game of my own going on. A teeny-weeny job here and Columbine's heart will swing once more towards yours truly.'

Harlequin gave a bow to no one in particular.

'But why tell?' asked Pete. 'Why tell me?'

'Like I said, my dear old chap, professional courtesy. The troupe will arrive tomorrow and not all of them look quite so favourably on wayward servants as I do.'

Harlequin spun on the tips of his toes, then dropped into a forward roll, springing up next to the table, his head level with Pete's wrinkled old ear.

'I'm here to tell you,' he whispered. 'That you need to run!'

— CHAPTER FIVE —

SEND IN THE CLOWNS

All anyone talked about at school the following day was the circus. The mysterious fate of everyone's craft projects barely registered on the school's radar. The only evidence of the previous evening's adventure was a makeshift sign on the swimming pool entrance, announcing that it was 'Closed for Cleaning'.

Lucy wondered if the school staff were getting used to covering things up too. They must be wondering what on earth was going on. Maybe Grandad's lot provided training for teachers who had to deal with kids like Lucy? Maybe that's what they did on inset days?

At lunchtime, Lucy went looking for Hobo. She wanted to apologise or, even better, just pick up as if nothing had happened. They were a team, after all. Lucy was sure he'd have forgiven her by now.

But Hobo wasn't in any of the usual places where

they met up. He was nowhere to be found. Lucy being Lucy, the first thing she suspected was foul play. Had the junk monster somehow pulled itself together and dragged its junk body out of the pool? Had there been more than one junk monster? But the truth was pretty obvious. Hobo was avoiding her.

And if she'd had any doubt, there were plenty of people ready to fill her in. In Ogmore-by-Sea, an art project could come to life and it would pass everyone by, but a row between Lucy and Hobo? If it hadn't been for the circus, it would have been the biggest news in town.

'Lost your alien, London?'

'Where's your pet?'

'Did the blob sit on you by mistake?'

'Finally got tired of hearing about the big city, did he?'

By the end of lunch, Lucy had come to the inescapable conclusion that it was much easier to be an outsider when there were two of you.

That afternoon was double English, and it offered a welcome escape. They were studying Shakespeare, hardly Lucy's favourite, but it kept the 'normals' off her back. She spent most of her time looking out of the window, hoping that Hobo might wander by on some special errand. Teachers always trusted Hobo.

But, of course, there was no such luck.

Five minutes before the end of the lesson, Mr Grant, Lucy's English teacher, normally so highbrow, joined the rest of the town in talking about the circus.

'Lucy's a bit of a clown, sir,' piped up Lucy's classmate, Hannah.

Lucy shot a venomous look at her. Mr Grant continued, seemingly oblivious: 'Clowning is, in fact, an old and proud tradition. Shakespeare himself made use of clowns in his plays, often to say things that no other character could possibly get away with saying. The role of the fool —'

'Lucy's one of them as well, sir!'

This time the laughter in the class was uncontrollable, and at the ring of the buzzer, Mr Grant stopped trying. Lucy sat and seethed, waiting for another wisecrack. Her cheeks, she knew, would be as red as any clown's.

As the rest of the class left, Mr Grant motioned that she should hang back.

'Look, sir,' she began, in no mood for his advice, no matter how well-meant.

Mr Grant cut her off by placing two tickets to the circus on the desk in front of her.

'I was going to give these as a prize today,' he said glumly. 'But you know this class – we never get to the end of a lesson. I think you should have them.'

'I'm not really the circus type, sir.'

'Well, from what I hear most of the town is going. People coming from Bridgend and Porthcawl, as well. Makes a change for us to be centre of attention. These tickets are for the front row, right in the middle. You should have them, take your friend Kostinen. Show them that you're not afraid of them.'

Lucy slipped the tickets into her satchel and shuffled out from behind the desk.

'Thanks, sir,' she said, forcing herself to smile. The tickets had probably been expensive. And even if she didn't want them, they were an olive branch for Hobo.

CHAPTER SIX

HOMECOMING

Lucy didn't catch the bus. She could see through the vehicle's windows that Hobo wasn't onboard, and she didn't fancy being the butt of any more of her classmates' jokes.

Her normal route home wouldn't have taken her past Hobo's house, but she fancied a walk anyway.

There were signs up for the circus everywhere. On lampposts, in shop windows, on the sides of bus shelters... Lucy couldn't turn a corner without coming face to face with a clown. They weren't traditional circus clowns either – there was something... *off* about them.

She stopped to stare at one of the larger posters on the side of a bus shelter. There was a clown dressed in white except for the big, black buttons and black trim on his coat. His face was also white, except for his black lips and a single black teardrop. There was a clown dressed as a military man, another as some sort of priest. There was a little fat one who wore a grotesque mask, and, front and centre, there was a Harlequin.

Lucy had owned a Harlequin doll when she was younger. She had no idea where it was now, and she would have been quite happy if it had been left behind in London.

'Coulrophobia,' said a voice in her ear, making her jump.

She turned around to find Hobo, distinctly non-clown-like despite his pale skin and bald head.

'Where did you spring from?' said Lucy, eager to gloss over the fact that he had startled her.

'Driving home with Dad, I spotted you staring at that poster. Thought for a minute you'd been taken over .'

'Came to my rescue, did you?'

'Thought perhaps you could use me. The Greater Intelligence.'

Lucy smiled. It seemed like she and Hobo were back on good terms.

'How come your dad was driving you?' she asked.

'Hospital appointment,' Hobo replied. 'Check up on the old alopecia.'

'Oh,' said Lucy, trying to sound disinterested – not like someone who had spent all day looking for a friend who she probably would have known had a hospital appointment if she'd paid attention in the first place.

'It's sold out,' said Hobo, breaking the awkward

silence between them. 'The circus.'

Lucy smiled. 'I can help with that,' she said, and rummaging in her satchel, pulled out the two tickets. She showed them to Hobo proudly. 'Courtesy of Mr Grant.'

Hobo took one of the tickets from Lucy and examined it carefully.

'What's wrong?' asked Lucy.

Hobo looked at her, his eyes narrowing. 'Have you forgotten what happened to us last time we were given tickets out of the blue? Free tickets to an exclusive event?'

Lucy felt something boil up inside of her. One minute, Hobo wanted nothing to do with her 'Lethbridge-Stewart stuff' and now here he was bringing it all up. Again.

'Forget it,' said Lucy, snatching the tickets back. 'You're probably right. It's certain death. Danger. Aliens! You wouldn't want to get involved.'

'Lucy, wait...' said Hobo.

But it was too late. Lucy was running.

On the other side of the road, Pete watched the girl and the bald boy talking. He heard their raised voices and, as she ran away, he could taste the salty taste of tears in the air. Pete could do that.

She was the *one*, he was sure of it.

He wondered if he should warn her. He

wondered if he could.

He wondered if she would believe him.

But all the while he could feel Harlequin's eyes on him, staring out from every poster. His eyes on every inch of this little town. Harlequin was watching. Harlequin was coming.

'No time,' muttered Pete to himself, dropping his head and continuing on his way.

Of course, it wasn't true. Pete had all the time in the world. It was just that there was a very real chance that 'all the time in the world' might run out that night, when the circus came to town.

Lucy slammed the front door shut behind her, tears still hot on her cheeks. She was about to disappear upstairs when she heard her mother's voice from the lounge.

'What do you mean, "you might be late back"? I've booked the restaurant.'

Mum was half shouting, half crying into the phone. Lucy stood in the doorway to the living room, watching as Mum paced back and forth, her eyes brimming with tears.

'No, Albert, you listen to me! You're the one who moved us down here, and now you're swanning off back in the opposite direction! Don't they care about you at all at work? Do they know you've got a family?'

Mum spotted Lucy standing in the doorway and immediately lowered her voice.

'Lucy's home. I suppose I've got to tell her?'

'Don't worry about it,' Lucy said, making a sharp exit. She took the stairs up to her bedroom two at a time and vanished into her room. She dived onto her bed and hid her head under her pillow as downstairs her mum turned the volume up to eleven. Lucy couldn't hear everything, but odd words filtered through, as if from a bad radio station.

'Work... Never here... Distracted... Priorities.'

Eventually things went quiet. Lucy waited for the inevitable creak of her mother climbing the stairs. When, finally, the door opened, her mum's cheeks were as tear-stained as her own. Lucy realised that they looked a lot alike when they cried.

'Lucy, I...'

'Don't worry, Mum, I heard.'

'Right, so...'

Lucy wondered if awkward silences were a 'Lethbridge-Stewart' thing as well.

'If there's anything I can do to make it up to you,' Mum offered weakly, perching herself on the edge of Lucy's bed. 'Anything you'd like to do?'

Lucy looked at her mum. She wanted to give her a break too.

Rolling over on the bed, Lucy reached down into the depths of her school satchel and retrieved the two now-slightly-crumpled circus tickets. She slid them across the bed to her mum.

'You're buying the popcorn, OK?'

Mum smiled. 'OK.'

'And the hot dogs.'

'OK.'

'And there might be candy floss.'

Mum winked away a tear. 'Don't push it, Lucy.'

— CHAPTER SEVEN —

A FIGURE IN THE DARK

Hobo watched from afar as Lucy and her mum headed into the circus. They didn't see him and he didn't try to get their attention. Instead he switched his attention to the rest of the crowd, all whispering excitedly as they walked into the Big Top.

Hobo's mum had been drafted from her Porthcawl beat for some extra patrols around Ogmore. Thieves sometimes targeted small towns when there was a big event on, knowing that houses would be empty. There were even cases where the thieves and circus troupe were one and the same. Despite not having a ticket, Hobo had asked his mum to drop him off so that he could have a look around, and she'd finally, grudgingly agreed. Hobo still hadn't earned back the trust he'd lost after disappearing to London with Lucy's family a few months ago. That was what Hobo had been trying, and failing, to explain to Lucy. You didn't have to be a Lethbridge-Stewart to have had your life turned upside down by the recent events.

Before he'd met Lucy, a trip to the library or half an hour on Wikipedia would sort out almost any predicament. To Hobo, knowledge really was power, and realising how little he really knew made him feel powerless.

Beating aliens was one thing; coming to terms with the fact that there were aliens in the first place, that was something else altogether.

Hobo joined the back of the crowd. There were some carnival games just inside the tent that looked like they didn't need a ticket. Nobody in the ambling crowd looked at Hobo, which was quite unusual in itself. He wondered if the legends of children running away to join the circus were based on kids like him – kids who were different, kids who were never going to fit in.

For a little while, he had thought he'd found somewhere he belonged – at Lucy's side. But while Lucy might be an outsider in Ogmore, she was part of something bigger now. Bigger than herself, bigger than Ogmore, and bigger than him.

All of a sudden Hobo felt eyes on him. He stopped, letting the crowd move away from him, and looked back into the darkness.

There was someone there. Someone in the dark,

staring at him.

'Who's there?' Hobo called out, his voice catching in his chest. His mind conjured up images of the criminal types his mum had warned him about. They were stalking towards him… Then they were pushed aside by a hoard of monsters and aliens gnashing their teeth. Hobo felt his heart pounding in his chest. The figure moved closer. The shape of it seemed all wrong in the darkness.

Hobo looked behind him. The last of the crowd had all but disappeared into the inner part of the tent. *No help then,* he thought. *Just me.*

'Come into the light,' stammered Hobo, turning back to face the figure. His hands went to his pockets, looking for something to defend himself with, but all he found was a wind-up torch, his house key on a novelty fob, some string, a pine cone, and his radio.

His radio.

He didn't know if Lucy would have hers with her, but he hoped desperately that she did. It was just a row after all; it wasn't like they'd fallen out forever.

'We're still a team,' Hobo whispered to himself as he pressed his thumb down hard on the send button, holding it there as the mysterious figure stepped forwards into the flickering lights of the circus.

CHAPTER EIGHT

BIG TOP

L ucy's tickets took her and Mum all the way to the front row.

'People are staring,' whispered Mum.

'Welcome to my world, Mum,' replied Lucy, taking no small degree of pleasure in passing a row of girls from her school. 'This is what it's like to be—'

'Don't say it,' said Mum.

Lucy raised an eyebrow. 'I was going to say Lucy Wilson.'

Lucy smiled as Mum laughed. It was good to see her happy again.

'These are our seats,' said Lucy, pointing to a pair of empty seats that undoubtedly had one of the best views in the whole place. They worked their way towards them, offering the customary 'sorry's' and 'excuse me's' to the people they passed, accepting in return each 'no problem', translating, of course, to 'why didn't you sit down already?'.

'And your teacher just gave these to you?' asked Mum, stowing her handbag under her seat and settling herself down.

'Yep,' replied Lucy.

'I'd have thought you'd be more suspicious of free tickets.'

Lucy screwed up her face. 'That's what Hobo said.'

'Is he here?' asked Mum, twisting around in her seat to scan the crowd. Even with most of Ogmore in attendance, she'd have had a decent chance of spotting him.

'Couldn't get a ticket,' replied Lucy flatly. She hadn't told her mum about her argument with Hobo. With everything else that was going on, she didn't really think it registered on the *Top 10 of Things Going Wrong* right now.

Lucy caught her mum looking at her, and realised her cover as blown.

'Not that I don't appreciate it, sweetheart, but is there a reason you didn't ask Hobo to come with you?'

'Long story,' replied Lucy, in the special tone that implied that the story, regardless of whether it was long or not, was not going to be told.

Pete stepped into the flickering light cast by the circus lamps.

Hobo breathed a sigh of relief. No monster. No alien. Just Punch and Judy Pete, hunchbacked and slow on his feet, lagging behind the crowd. Hobo let go of the send button on his radio and offered a silent prayer that Lucy hadn't heard him making a fool of himself.

'Er, hi,' said Hobo sheepishly. 'Sorry about that. You, er… startled me, I guess. You're Pete, the guy who runs the Punch and Judy down by the beach, right?'

'Afraid of dark, eh?' grunted Pete. 'Wise boy. Light is safest here.'

'Sorry, what?' said Hobo. 'What do you mean?'

Moving far faster than his crooked old frame suggested, Pete closed the distance between himself and Hobo. He prodded a finger sharply into Hobo's stomach.

'Soft,' he said. 'Too soft. Where is girl?'

Hobo took a step back, stumbling slightly. His hand wrapped around the radio again, fumbling for the send button.

'Girl? You mean Lucy?'

'Girl,' said Pete, waving his arms at the circus. 'The girl. All this for the girl!

'Oh no,' whispered Hobo. 'It's happening again, isn't it? Are you with them? With UNIT?'

'No,' interrupted Pete, pushing past Hobo with a strength that was as surprising as his speed. 'I am clown.'

Hobo chased after him, struggling to keep up. He

felt his heart pounding in his chest. Lucy was in trouble. Again.

'Clown? You mean with this circus or…?'

The old man wasn't listening. Hobo pulled the radio out of his pocket.

'Lucy? It's me, can you hear me? I'm outside the circus! There's someone here, he says he's with the circus. Or maybe something called CLOWN? It doesn't matter. He says this whole thing is for you, Lucy. The circus is here for you! It's a trap!'

— CHAPTER NINE —

AN UNWILLING
VOLUNTEER

The lights dimmed in the Big Top, and a drum roll filled the air like thunder. Spotlights ran over the faces of crowd, before settling to a single spot in the middle of the tent.

The drums fell silent. The crowd waited.

In the spotlight a figure was crouched. Swathed in a dark cloak, it was perfectly motionless. Every man, woman and child in the crowd held their breath.

Seconds. Ticked. By.

And then dark cloak flew upwards, seemingly vanishing into thin air, and Harlequin was revealed. Illuminated by the spotlight, his patchwork outfit sparkled. He lifted his head to the crowd, the long nose of his mask pointing upwards and his painted lips curling in a half-smile, half-sneer. He raised a hand; the crowd took a single breath.

Lucy found herself sitting forward in her seat, as if a magnetic force were drawing her towards the stage. Whilst everyone else in the place seemed entranced by Harlequin, her mind itched at the sight of him. There was something wrong, something out of place. Otherworldly, that was the word. Otherworldly. From another world.

Alien.

Suddenly Harlequin spoke.

'Welcome, one and all, to the show!'

Music blared, jerking the crowd from their trance. From all sides, clowns appeared. Cartwheeling, tumbling, skipping, jumping, running, they began to fill the Big Top. Some moved through the crowd, eliciting laughter and excited cheers from the circus-goers. Lucy sat back in her chair. It was just an act. A performance.

Mum lent across to her. 'They're a bit… different, aren't they, love?'

'I think they're from Europe, Mum.'

'Ooh,' said Mum. Despite her London upbringing, there was still something about things 'from Europe' that she seemed to find deeply exotic.

The clowns began to line up by type, forming ranks around Harlequin.

'Ladies and gentleman,' crooned Harlequin, 'allow me to introduce our players!'

He bowed to the nearest rank, and a group of clowns stepped forwards, the spotlights swinging towards them. They were all dressed in identical tight-fitting red costumes, long dark coats, and strange, pointed yellow slippers. They had masks too, but not like Harlequin's. These masks all had moustaches or beards, which made the clowns look like old men.

One of them stepped forwards. This one's outfit seemed slightly grander than the others, stitched with golden thread that shone under the glare of the spotlights.

'This man is a Pantalone!' shouted Harlequin, bowing to the clown. 'People of fair Ogmore-by-Sea, watch out for the Pantalones! They are wealthy men and great admirers of the ladies.'

On cue, the Pantalones pulled bunches of fake flowers from inside their dark overcoats and went leaping and cavorting into the crowd, dishing the flowers out to all the women they could find. Lucy hung her head in raw, searing embarrassment as Mum smiled and giggled when presented with a bunch of paper roses. Her clown suitor fell tumbling backwards away from her, to be rescued by some of his comrades.

'You're right,' Mum whispered to Lucy. 'Definitely European.'

The show continued with each group of clowns introduced in turn. The Capitanos were a sort of mock soldier in oversized boots and comedy uniforms, who challenged various men and boys in the audience to strength tests; they either lost spectacularly or backed out as soon as their challenge was accepted. The Brighellas were dressed in white and green, and Harlequin described them as brigands and thieves; they took great pleasure in pretending to rob various members of the audience. The Dottores seemed to be dressed as priests, but Mum said they were scholars; they seemed mostly to fuss with the other clowns, telling them off for their antics.

The whole thing was dragging on a bit for Lucy. Where were all the strong men, the trapeze artists? At least there were no animal acts. She could not bare that. Then Harlequin finally reached the end of his seemingly endless introductions.

'And now,' he intoned, 'Ladies and Gentlemen, you have met our players, and our show can truly begin.'

The crowd cheered. From the far back someone shouted, 'About time,' earning a fierce glare from Harlequin.

'No respect for the arts,' muttered Mum.

Lucy smiled. *My mum, the theatre critic*, she thought.

'Without further ado,' said Harlequin, a slight edge in his voice, 'we begin with the one thing that all circuses have, and the one thing that no circus can do without… magic!'

From somewhere outside the Big Top, a pair of Dottores wheeled in a large box. It was blue, about the size of a telephone box, and speckled with moons and stars.

'This box,' said Harlequin, pointing one long finger at it, 'is magic itself. With this special box you can make anything disappear! Perhaps a man, perhaps a woman, perhaps a boy, perhaps a girl…'

Harlequin began to prowl towards the audience, his eyes like spotlights of their own, searching the crowd. He began to tip toe and pirouette towards where Lucy was sitting.

Lucy edged down in her seat. *Just for once*, she thought. *Please let someone else be the one who gets singled out.* She shut her eyes, willing the clown to move on, to pick someone else.

'All we need is a volunteer!'

A cheer went up, followed by a flood of applause. Lucy realised she had been holding her breath, and she took a deep lungful of air as she opened her eyes. Then she let it all out again in a gasp. Harlequin was there, right there, right in front of her.

And he was holding Mum by the hand.

Hobo caught up with Pete a yard or so away from the Big Top.

There were two large, stocky clowns blocking the entrance flap, dressed in strange military-style uniforms. They turned slowly to face Pete. They were wearing masks, just like all the other clowns, but no mask could have concealed the malice radiating from their eyes.

'Clown,' hissed one of them.

Hobo looked around frantically, searching for a way to get to Lucy. With a cracking sound, like someone tipping out a box of dominoes, Pete straightened himself up to his full height. He was head and shoulders taller than Hobo, and broader too.

'I am clown,' he said. His voice was much stronger than it had been before, and he spoke now with a different accent. 'I am clown. You will let me pass!'

The other clowns didn't answer. From somewhere inside their puffy sleeves, long and slender truncheons slipped down into their hands. They spread apart, flanking the old man and Hobo, their eyes flaring in the darkness.

'What's going on? Who are you?' asked Hobo, forced closer to Pete by the advance of the clowns.

'I am clown,' he replied. 'They will let me pass.'

Hobo took the hint and charged for the Big Top entrance. The clowns didn't stop him, and as he passed through the flap and into the darkness beyond, he heard the sickening sounds of truncheons smashing down over and over again.

*

'Oh gosh, this is so embarrassing,' said Mum, climbing awkwardly over the low wooden barrier that separated the crowd from the Big Top proper.

'Who for?' hissed Lucy, desperately beckoning for her mum to come back to her seat. 'Mum, everyone's watching!'

'I know!' said Mum, smiling and waving to the crowd. There were cheers and claps. Someone wolf-whistled. 'Nothing like this ever happened back in London, did it?'

Lucy watched as Harlequin led her mum across the sawdust-covered floor towards the shiny blue box. She wanted to shut her eyes again, shut her eyes and cover her ears and just wait for it all to be over. Not that it ever would be. School on Monday was going to be a nightmare after this.

'Lucy!'

Lucy turned in her seat as Hobo came charging down the aisle.

'Hobo? What are you doing?'

'Trap…' gasped Hobo, trying to catch his breath. 'It's a trap, Lucy. The circus. It's here for you!'

Lucy's eyes grew wide.

'Hobo, they've got Mum!'

Harlequin was parading Mum around in a circle like a prize pony, showing her off to the crowd.

Vaulting over the wooden barricade, Lucy made

a run for the middle of the Big Top, towards her mum and Harlequin.

'Lucy? What are you doing?' shouted Hobo.

'Saving Mum!'

Had Lucy looked back, she might have seen the clowns slipping from the shadows and grabbing Hobo firmly by the arms. She might have seen Hobo struggling, fighting, desperately trying to get free.

But she didn't look back.

Instead, she kept her eyes dead ahead. She threw herself in between Mum and Harlequin and stood defiantly in front of the gaudy, multi-coloured clown.

'You don't want her,' said Lucy, her voice as brave as it had ever been. 'You want me.'

Harlequin bent gracefully at the waist, bringing his masked face level with Lucy's, his long nose brushing her cheek, his lips almost touching her ear.

'And now,' he whispered. 'I have you.'

— CHAPTER TEN —
BIG BLUE BOX

'Lucy? What's going on?' asked Mum. 'You're making a show of us.'

'Tell Mummy,' hissed Harlequin, 'to get back in her seat.'

Lucy turned to face her mum. Behind her she could see the crowd, laughing and pointing and jeering. She could see the space where Hobo should have been. Now she was getting worried.

'I really want to do this, Mum,' said Lucy, her voice quavering. 'Show them I'm not afraid.'

Mum smiled. For a split second Lucy thought she was going to give her a peck on the cheek, but instead she took two steps backwards. Normally Lucy would have been glad, but at the moment a kiss from her mum would have been very welcome.

'Back to your seat then, Mum, yeah?'

'All right, dear, back to my seat! You knock 'em dead!'

Mum turned and was escorted from the stage by two of the Dottore clowns, who seemed to appear from nowhere. Lucy watched her go, and when she was seated safely, Lucy turned once more to face Harlequin.

'I don't know who, or what, you are,' she said sternly, 'but I'm Lucy Wilson. My grandfather was Brigadier Lethbridge-Stewart. I beat the Great Intelligence. I'll beat you.'

Harlequin smiled, revealing a row of pointed teeth that looked like they belonged in the mouth of some deep-sea creature.

'And now…' he intoned to the crowd, 'you will marvel. You will be amazed. You will be awed by the magic on display. I am about to make this girl disappear!'

Harlequin walked backwards, spinning and twisting as he did so, and grabbed Lucy roughly by the hand. He half-walked, half-dragged her over to the box, flinging open the doors. Lucy could see that in the box was lined from floor to ceiling with mirrors. Even the ceiling and floors had mirrors on them. A tiny hall of mirrors, it looked like it went on forever, though in reality it was nothing but a box.

A big, blue box.

Something sparked in Lucy's memory. An image, a memory: sitting on her grandfather's lap, in his favourite chair, listening to his stories. Something about a box. Something about a strange man, a man with more than once face. Always familiar, but alien at the same time. A rule. He'd made her repeat it, even though she hadn't understood it at the time.

'Don't go into the big blue box.'

Harlequin shoved Lucy hard in the small of the back, and she stumbled forwards into the box. She found herself surrounded by mirror images of herself, different Lucys from different angles, repeating endlessly away from her. All of them had tears at the corners of their eyes. All of them looked angry and afraid.

'Goodbye, dear,' said Harlequin, bowing low as the doors slammed shut.

Lucy felt the box spinning. They must have been spinning it around outside. She'd seen this trick done before, on television. There would be a trap door in the floor, or in the back of the box.

She ran her hands along a mirror, where the gap for the doors should have been. But there was nothing but perfectly smooth glass. No gap, no join. Nothing but mirrors and endless Lucy Wilsons.

'Trapped,' she muttered. 'Sorry, Grandad.'

Grandad. Lucy had barely spoken the word when it happened. A hot, fizzing sensation on her hand, coming from the ring she had been given by Grandad's friend, Dame Anne Bishop. She looked down at it. It wasn't much to look at: just a thin strip of metal with an opaque stone. Holding her hand up close to her face, Lucy examined it closer.

'What do you do?' she said. The ring didn't answer.

Suddenly the spinning stopped. Lucy braced herself. Maybe she hadn't been spinning. Maybe the box had been taken somewhere. Maybe it had taken *her* somewhere. Aliens had to have a way of getting about – maybe this was it.

'Stop being stupid,' Lucy said to herself sternly. 'Think. You've got to get out of here.'

She began to search again. She checked the floor, then the ceiling. No trap doors, no hidden catches. She checked where the doors had been again, but still she could find nothing. She turned around and around, making herself dizzy, desperately looking for something, anything... but there was nothing.

As Lucy slid down to the floor, she realised that, one by one, her reflections were disappearing. Lucy pressed her hands against the glass, scrambling to try and keep hold, somehow, of herself. Then she realised that her reflection didn't seem to even be *her* reflection anymore.

It didn't move when she moved. It moved on its own. All around her, Lucy's reflections turned to look down at her. They banged their hands noiselessly against the glass. They waved, gesticulated, and opened their mouths in silent, desperate screams. Lucy watched in horror as her panicking reflections tried to reach out for one another, as they pointed in terror at whatever invisible force they could sense was coming for them.

One by one, they vanished.

Harlequin was right. The box was magic and, bit by bit, Lucy Wilson was disappearing.

CHAPTER ELEVEN

WAKING UP A CLOWN

Lucy woke up in bed with a headache. It was morning, or at least it felt like morning, but her eyes wouldn't focus properly, and she couldn't read the clock by the side of her bed. Her mouth felt like it was full of cotton wool.

She closed her eyes and tried to fall back to sleep, but her bed felt hot and damp, and her head wouldn't stop spinning. Lucy couldn't remember the last time she'd had a nightmare like that. Even after London, even after the Great Intelligence and everything that had followed, she'd slept just as soundly as she ever did.

Maybe then she'd just been exhausted. Maybe this was how her life would be, and some crazy dream about clowns and mirrors was just the start of it.

Lucy half rolled, half fell out of bed, and staggered across the room to her dressing table. She clicked on a little lamp and started to scream.

She screamed because on her bed behind her,

wearing her pyjamas and cuddling the teddy bear that she had brought all the way from London – but denied knowing anything about – another Lucy was fast asleep.

She screamed because when she looked in the mirror she was still Lucy, but her face was hidden beneath a deep cake of make-up. White make-up, red make-up, black make-up. Plaster white over her whole face, black lines around her eyes that ran down to little black teardrops, red on her lips and on the tip of her nose.

Lucy screamed because the clowns and the mirrors really had been just the start of it.

She screamed because no matter how much she did scream, nobody seemed to hear her.

Lucy staggered away from her dressing table to the corner of the room. The thing in the bed, the thing with her face, was still fast asleep. She tried to take stock of her situation: she was there, she was dressed, she could feel the floor beneath her boots and her back against the wall. But somehow... somehow she knew that she had become disconnected from the world. She felt a step out of sync with everything, like she'd tuned out in the middle of a conversation and was now trying to catch up. She was unfocused, fuzzy, like the grainy old videos they watched in History class.

She thought about the mirrors inside the big blue

box. The box she should never have got inside, the box her grandfather had warned her about. She thought about the other Lucys, disappearing one by one. Her ring felt hot on her finger again, hot and itchy. At least that was something, something that felt real. She felt like it was the ring that was holding her in place somehow – that it was her anchor in the world.

'I need Hobo,' Lucy said to herself. 'And I need to get Mum out of here.'

Slowly, she started to edge towards the door. All she had to do was to get past the thing that wasn't Lucy, then down to the landing and into Mum's bedroom. After London, she wouldn't need to explain; she could just get them out of the house and then work out what to do.

Lucy was halfway to the door when it opened. Lucy froze, covering her mouth.

Mum stood in the doorway, holding a breakfast tray. 'Lucy, wake up! Your father's made breakfast!'

— CHAPTER TWELVE —
HARLEQUIN'S RAGE

The circus was still in town but Harlequin was in no laughing mood.

'Take it apart!' he roared, spittle flying from between his razor sharp teeth. 'Take it apart and find the girl! Put its insides on its outsides! Unmake it, remake it, then unmake it again!'

A group of Dottores stood around Harlequin's blue box, shuffling their feet nervously.

'Well?'

One Dottore, braver or perhaps more stupid than the rest, broke away from the pack and approached Harlequin. He moved slowly, cautiously, in the way a man might approach a dangerous animal.

'Your lordship,' he said, bowing low. 'The machine is not a thing to simply be taken apart and put back together again. The mechanism is complex. Whatever the girl did, I assure you we will find the remedy, but we must have more time.'

Harlequin paced back and forth, his hands twisting and turning in the air as if he were operating some secret and invisible machine of his own – or simply looking for something to strangle. Eventually, he was still. The Dottore stood, trembling, before his lord.

'Time,' said Harlequin, his voice low and calm. 'Why is it always about time?'

'The girl will not elude us,' said the Dottore.

Harlequin raised a single finger, silencing the clown. Something electric moved through the air, something dark and greasy and fearful. The clowns all held their breath, as entranced as the crowd had been the night before. They all knew that when Harlequin next spoke, there was a very good chance that it would be the last thing that any of them would ever hear.

'Did you know,' he began, 'that when I was a young man my true love spurned me? The Lady Columbine, can you imagine? Stolen! How I cried, my dear Dottore. How I wept. And how I asked myself, again and again, what is wrong with Harlequin?'

The tall, patchwork-covered clown paused, his eyes fixed on the Dottore in front of him. The dark, electrical energy moved behind his eyes. The other Dottores began to shuffle backwards, led by one whose beard was a little longer than the rest. An older Dottore, he had seen this Harlequin show before.

He knew how it ended.

'Err, nothing, my lord,' suggested the isolated Dottore weakly. 'There is nothing wrong with you, of course.'

'Nothing?' replied Harlequin, his voice dripping with sarcasm. 'Surely you cannot mean that our Lady Columbine was mistaken then? That her heart, her very heart, the purest and most loving of all hearts, spoke untruthfully?'

'No, no, my lord, of course not, I simply meant... well that is to say...'

Harlequin skipped nimbly forwards and placed his hand gently on the clown's shoulder, dipping his head to his ear.

'Don't stammer, my darling,' he whispered. 'You'll ruin the performance.'

Pirouetting away before the clown could answer, Harlequin reached behind himself, slipping his hand into an almost invisible seam in the back of his patchwork costume. He pulled out a blade – of sorts. It was so sharp that it cut the light that hit it. It was so sharp that it seemed almost to be cutting its way out of this world and into another, leaving only the handle behind.

It was less of 'a' blade and more of 'the' blade, the blade from which all other blades had been born. Harlequin spun the handle of the blade on the tip of an outstretched finger, and around it swirled a splintered kaleidoscope of mirror images.

'My lord, my lord, I beg of you, please,' stammered the Dottore.

'I asked myself the same question. What is wrong with Harlequin? And I must confess, much like you, my friend, I could not conceive an answer. I racked my brains, but no answer would come. And yet, I knew my love could not be wrong.'

Harlequin paused for a moment. The remaining Dottores had inched, shuffled and crept to the edge of the tent. They waited beside a thin flap of canvas, the only thing between them and escape. But they could not have been more trapped if the tent had been made of iron. Harlequin always had to have an audience.

'Do you know how I answered my question, dear Dottore?'

'My lord, I...'

Harlequin sighed. 'For such a learned man, you seem to know very little. Perhaps it's because you look for knowledge in your dusty old books, whereas I have looked within.'

On tiptoe, Harlequin prowled towards the Dottore, the blade balanced delicately on his finger.

'I took myself apart,' Harlequin continued. 'Piece by piece. Part by part. Slice by slice. I looked at how I worked. I looked at how I was broken. And then I put myself back together.'

'My lord, please,' said the clown with a gasp. The blade was so close now, the whirling mirror fragments all reflecting the Dottore's face, twisting and contorting it, unmaking the clown before his own eyes.

Harlequin smiled, baring his razor teeth.

'I lost a few pieces in the process, I think,' he hissed. 'That's why I have so many patches.'

— CHAPTER THIRTEEN —

BREAKFAST TIME

Not-Lucy stirred and opened her eyes, a smile slowly spreading across her face.

First mistake, thought Lucy. *I'm never happy first thing in the morning, breakfast in bed or not.*

But Not-Lucy was relentlessly cheerful. She threw back the covers and stretched as she sat up, beaming away the whole time.

'I had the most amazing dream, Mum.'

Lucy winced. Not-Lucy sounded just like her, but saccharine sweet. She was the kids' breakfast cereal edition of Lucy. Mum didn't seem to notice. She beamed back the same two-hundred-watt, two-thousand-calorie smile.

'That's nice, Lucy,' she replied, gently placing the breakfast tray down on the bed.

'Mum!' Lucy tried to shout, but just like with her scream, no one seemed to hear her.

She watched as Not-Lucy ate her food, before getting out of bed and neatly placing her tray out on the floor of the landing. Then her doppelganger turned around and just got back into bed. Lucy watched as the thing sat there, motionless, its eyes vacant, staring straight ahead. Seconds, then minutes ticked by, and still the thing didn't move. It was as if it had simply run out of ideas what to do next.

'It's Monday. You need to get ready for school, dummy,' said Lucy sullenly.

When she spoke this time, it felt different. Maybe it was because she wasn't shouting anymore. Maybe it was because her ring, the strange little ring, felt like it was whizzing and whirring around on her finger. A dial tuning into some unknown frequency. Whatever the reason, the words did their work.

'It's Monday,' repeated Not-Lucy, 'I need to get ready for school.'

The thing swung its legs off the bed, grabbed Lucy's towel and wash bag from a hook on the back of the bedroom door, and headed out of the room. Lucy gave chase, but by the time she'd reached the landing, the thing was already in the bathroom and had locked the door behind it.

'OK,' Lucy said to herself. 'So that thing can hear me, but it looks like nobody else can. What else can I do?'

She crept along the landing to the bathroom door. Listening carefully, she could hear the Not-Lucy running water, preparing for whatever it was that mysterious alien doppelgangers did in the bathroom.

'Keep it up, dummy,' said Lucy. 'Definitely nothing weird going on out here for you to worry about.'

Tentatively, Lucy reached out and pressed against the door with her fingertips. Still locked, and still as solid as ever. Lucy let out a sigh.

'OK, so no walking through walls,' she confirmed to herself. 'Not a ghost then. So what am I?'

Lucy wished her memories of her grandfather were clearer, more organised. It seemed obvious now that all his old stories hadn't just been for her amusement. They were instructions. They were training. Maybe if Lucy's father hadn't turned his back on the 'family business', then maybe Lucy would have had more to work with than half-remembered memories of the old brigadier's shaggy dog stories. Maybe she would know what to do.

A creak on the stairs startled her, and Lucy instinctively ducked out of sight. Peeping through the banister, she could see Mum at the bottom of the staircase. But she was not alone. Just behind her, its hand resting gently on her shoulder, was a clown.

Tall and thin, it was dressed in yellow and white, its face painted and covered in a half mask. The hand not resting on Mum's shoulder was holding a wilting bunch of flowers.

'Pantalone,' whispered Lucy.

The clown looked up, its masked eyes landing on Lucy, and she realised she knew exactly what to do.

She had to run.

— CHAPTER FOURTEEN —

THE IMPORTANCE OF BEING INVISIBLE

Pete opened up his Punch and Judy show at the same time every morning except Christmas Day, when he had a lie-in for an hour.

Technically, Pete didn't need to sleep, but he enjoyed the convention of lying down in the dark at the end of a busy day. Also, staying up all night with the lights on was the kind of thing that set tongues in a small town wagging – and that simply would not do. Banality had been the cornerstone of his plan when he had first arrived here. Humans quickly learned to ignore things that they saw everyday. Even the quirkiest of occurrences could soon become familiar, boring, if repeated every day.

Being invisible was how Pete had survived a war so great and terrible that the shockwaves had been felt on a hundred different worlds. In some parts of the universe the war had ended long ago; in others it still raged. In some, it was yet to begin; and these places were most dangerous of all.

Pete had survived, was surviving, and would survive in the future too. All he had to do was stay invisible.

But that was going to be hard with half the town outside his booth. Mothers, fathers, grandparents, children, teenagers, babies, and clowns.

Everyone had a clown.

They stood in the crowd, one clown for every person, all perfectly invisible yet all terrifyingly real. They whispered things, the clowns. Pete knew their language. He heard the things they said, and he watched as the people unwittingly obeyed. They sat, as one, as Pete drew back the tiny curtains that framed the miniature stage at the front of the booth. They clapped, as one, as Pete raised his puppets up into view. And, of course, they laughed.

In the entire universe, there is no sound more guaranteed to chill the blood than the laughter of clowns.

Lucy raced down the landing and back into her bedroom, kicking the door shut behind her. She knew she only had a few moments. She had to spend them wisely.

Reaching under the bed, she pulled out her 'Go Bag'. A tip from Grandad that she had remembered: always have a bag of essentials packed. It had been a good excuse not to unpack properly after London. Now it could be the difference between life and death.

Swinging the bag onto her shoulder, Lucy grabbed her radio from her dressing table and a heavy jacket from the back of the door.

Footsteps on the landing.

A faint sound. Hissing. Whispering. Then her mother's voice.

'Come out, Lucy.'

Lucy grabbed the foot of her bed and heaved, pulling it across the floor to block the door. Then she ran to the window, pulled the curtains open and unhooked the old sash. Outside, clouds with dark bellies lurked overhead. When Lucy had first come to Ogmore, she'd fantasised about running away. In her dreams, the weather had always been better.

'Lucy, where are you?' asked Mum plaintively.

'I'm not here,' said Lucy. 'Sorry, Mum.'

Behind Lucy, her bedroom door clunked against the impromptu bed-barricade. She didn't know if her mum could hear her. But she knew the clown could. It had seen her, and it had sent Mum in pursuit.

Lucy swung her leg up and out of the window. Her bedroom was at the front of the house, her window only a foot a so above the tiled roof of the porch. She clambered out, carefully putting her weight onto the roof. The ghost of every chocolate bar, packet of crisps, and plate of chips threatened to thwart her escape, but Lucy had a gymnast's build and the skills that went with it. She leapt confidently off the roof, landing on the small patch of grass next to the path.

She could hear footsteps thundering down the stairs within the house. Lucy headed straight for the garden wall, vaulted it, and ran as fast as she could down the road.

She didn't look back.

For all she knew, she would never see her home or her family again.

Hobo was having a strange morning.

First, there had been the dream. He'd woken up fully dressed, soaked with sweat, his bed clothes tight around him like a shroud, and his heart pounding in his chest, faster than he'd ever felt it beat before. His brain, meanwhile, was filled with one thing, one thought, looping over and over.

Clowns.

Hobo had had nightmares before. When his alopecia first manifested itself, he'd had nightmares about his hair falling out. They only stopped when the last wispy strands had fallen away. And when the nightmare became real, the feeling left over by it no longer had any power over him.

But last night's nightmare had been unlike any Hobo had had before. It was more real, more fantastic, utterly clear. And however bad it had been, Hobo was somehow sure that the world he had woken up into was far worse again.

All of which simply didn't fit with the second strange thing that morning – the news. Hobo and Lucy might have sworn off mobile phones to protect themselves against the influence of the Great Intelligence, but an information junkie like Hobo could never give up his Internet connection. Protected by more firewalls than the biggest corporations, Hobo's laptop was his link to the rest of the world. Lucy had her 'intuition', her cosmic link with the strange and the alien, handed down from her grandfather. Hobo had his news. Sorted, searched, and filtered, Hobo's news feed was tuned towards those same strange and alien things that Lucy was attuned to. Hobo called it his 'Early Warning System'.

The Early Warning System always had news, even if it wasn't the news Hobo and Lucy were looking for.

'The problem,' Hobo had explained to Lucy, 'is that the world is full of strange and unusual things.'

'That's why aliens like it here. Easy to hide.'

'Exactly. Like hiding a tree in a forest.'

But today there was nothing to report.

Literally, nothing.

Hobo sat at his laptop, still in last night's clothes, scouring Google. At first he thought it was just his system that was broken, but after a while, after search after search came back empty, he reached a different conclusion. According to every news source in the world, there was nothing happening on planet Earth. Nothing at all.

'All is well,' Hobo muttered to himself. 'All is well.'

And things had continued to be well for the rest of the morning. All was well at breakfast, where Hobo's mother reported that crime was at an all time low, and where his father read aloud from the morning paper a glowing review of the circus, which was extending its stay in town. All was well when Hobo left to catch the bus to school, and all was well as he waited for the bus to arrive.

He was used to being different and he had plenty of friends who treated him the same as any other human, but there were the others. The ones who picked on him because of his bald head and maybe the brain inside it too. A minority but it was hard to escape them. These Neanderthals would routinely offer a jibe, a barb, or outright insult. 'The Blob', 'The Freak'… He'd heard it all. Why didn't the bullies in Ogmore own a thesaurus? But today was different. Today kids just said, 'Hello'. They said, 'Hi'. One even tried to high five him so unexpectedly that Hobo initially thought the kid was going to punch him.

At the bus stop, *all was well*, and that was what tipped the balance.

Hobo could ignore a bad dream. He could ignore a weird bug on his laptop. He could ignore a day where there was no news at all. He could ignore tumbling crime figures, or a circus that was mysteriously not only better than any other show on the planet, but could also be sustained by the populace of one small Welsh town.

But he couldn't ignore kids suddenly… not being kids. Hobo had learned the hard way that one thing that could always be relied upon was the cruelty of other children.

He remembered the words he had once said to Lucy with such conviction: 'Guard your mind'. And, as he said them to himself, in his own head, the strangest thing in a morning of strange things revealed itself.

Somebody, an invisible somebody, was whispering to Hobo.

— CHAPTER FIFTEEN —
EVERYONE HAS
A CLOWN

Lucy kept running until her lungs felt like two fireballs burning through her chest. Wheezing, she ducked into a lane behind a row of houses and stopped. Her legs were shaking, and as she caught her breath, she realised she wasn't sure where she was. She hadn't had a destination in mind when she'd run away. 'Anywhere but here,' was as far as she'd thought things through.

'Anywhere but here,' she said to herself, resting her back against the brick wall of the lane. 'Great plan, Lucy.'

A car passed on the road, and on reflex Lucy ducked deeper into the lane. She watched as another car went past – one driver, one passenger, and two clowns. Another car, then another. Every car had a clown. Everyone had a clown.

'It's not just me,' said Lucy to herself. 'It's not just me!'

But if everyone in Ogmore had a clown, then *everyone* was in danger. Everyone, including Paula and Maya and all her friends with normal-sized brains, but Hobo most of all. The one person Lucy could rely on when things got weird and dangerous.

Lucy pulled her radio out of her pocket and pressed the transmit button.

'Hobo, can you hear me?'

She waited. Seconds stretched themselves out like elastic, taut, ready to snap.

'Hobo, are you there?'

'Lucy?'

'Hobo! Thank goodness you're OK. Wait, *are* you OK? Where are you? Are you somewhere safe?'

'I'm on the school bus,' said Hobo. He sounded confused, a little anxious too. 'We're just about to get to your stop. I have lots to tell you about.'

'Hobo, listen, you're not safe, nobody's safe! We need to meet *somewhere safe*. You understand?'

Somewhere safe – Lucy had laughed at Hobo when he had come up with the idea of a pre-agreed secret rendezvous point, but she was not laughing now.

'Lucy,' replied Hobo, 'what are you on about?'

'The clowns, Hobo! The clowns!'

'Very funny, Lucy,' said Hobo, sarcastically. 'Just get on the bus.'

'What do you mean? I'm not at the bus stop.'

'Lucy, give it up! I can see you. Hang on, how are

you talking to me? Where's your radio?'

Lucy almost dropped her radio, her hands suddenly trembling. She jammed her thumb hard against the transmission button.

'Hobo, stay away from her! She's not me! She is *not* me!'

Lucy waited. She waited for her hands to stop shaking. She waited for the sudden sick feeling that had surged up from her stomach to go back down again. She waited for the tears she could feel at the corners of her eyes to vanish. And she waited to hear back from Hobo, which was the one thing that never came.

Lucy stuffed the radio back in her pocket. Creeping to the end of the lane, she peeped out and got her bearings. A street away from Hobo's place. She'd run further than she'd thought. Maybe she'd had a destination in mind after all.

'I'm coming, Hobo,' said Lucy, tightening the straps of her rucksack and zipping up her jacket.

Whether he liked it or not, Hobo Kostinen was neck deep in Lethbridge-Stewart stuff.

'Nice radio, mate, let's have a go!'

Hobo didn't recognise the boy leaning over from behind him, or react quickly enough to stop the boy from taking the radio out of his hand.

'Wow, this is awesome!'

'I'm going to need that back,' Hobo protested, reaching for the radio as the boy passed it to a friend further back. 'I need to speak to Lucy.'

'I'm Lucy.'

Hobo turned and found himself face to face with Lucy.

Except, it wasn't Lucy. It looked like her, sounded like her, but it wasn't her. Her uniform was neat; her hair was clipped, and was that… *make-up*? The real Lucy never used make-up, had only limited control over her hair, and wore her uniform as if it had just been retrieved from lost properly. Even without the conversation over the radio, Hobo would have known something was up.

The question now was what kind of something?

'I'm Lucy,' Not-Lucy said again.

'I beg to differ,' replied Hobo. 'Whoever you are, whatever you are, you're not Lucy Wilson.'

'I'm not Lucy Wilson.'

A tap on the shoulder made Hobo turn. The kid with the sudden enthusiasm for radios was smiling sheepishly at him.

'Sorry, mate,' he said, holding up the shattered remains of Hobo's radio. 'One of the lads dropped it.'

Hobo snatched the radio back. He didn't know this kid; could he be another sub-par doppelganger? Was the entire bus full of replacements? Hobo wished he'd paid more attention to his schoolmates, but all they had ever done was bully him.

'We all thought it was really cool though,' the kid continued. 'Everyone was wondering where you got it, and if anyone else has one. I told them somebody must do, because you were talking to them.'

'Yeah, sure, whatever,' replied Hobo. It had occurred to him that if the whole bus might be replacements, or whatever Not-Lucy was, it was best to act natural, like he hadn't noticed a thing. He shoved the broken radio down into his bag, burying it under his school books, and turned to face the front of the bus.

The kid grabbed him by the shoulder again, twisting him back around.

'We all want to know who else has one,' he said, his voice now oozing with the kind of menace Hobo was used to from his peers. 'And we want to know where she is.'

'She's right there,' replied Hobo, pointing to Not-Lucy, who was still standing in the aisle of the bus. 'That's who I was talking to.'

'I'm not Lucy Wilson,' said Not-Lucy, seemingly excited to be part of the conversation.

'That's right,' said Hobo, thinking on his feet. 'You're Lucy Lethbridge-Stewart. And you need to sit down.'

'I need to sit down,' said Not-Lucy, popping

herself down next to Hobo and straightening her uniform.

Through the window, Hobo could see that they were finally pulling up outside the school. Assuming he could slip away as everyone got off the bus, he could rendezvous with the real Lucy in less than half an hour. All he had to do was escape.

'Boys and girls, your attention please.'

Hobo craned his neck to see what was going on. It was Mr Grant, one of the English teachers. What was he doing on the bus?

'As a special treat,' continued Mr Grant, 'the school has arranged for you all to go on a trip this morning. You'll all be heading down to the beach.'

Mr Grant paused as the bus filled with cheers.

'And then... settle down now... and then you will all have the privilege of seeing the Punch and Judy show!'

The bus erupted into a cacophony of raucous approval, as the driver closed the doors and pulled away. Hobo watched the school, and his chance of escape, disappear behind them.

'I'm Lucy Lethbridge-Stewart,' said the impostor sitting next to Hobo.

'I wish you were,' he replied. 'I really wish you were.'

*

Lucy had made better time than she'd expected,

arriving just in time to see the bus pull away.

Through the window she'd seen Hobo talking to her freakish doppelganger. She'd watched as the thing had sat down next to him, in her seat next to him, as the bus pulled away. And she'd watched the clowns. Like everywhere else, where there were people, there were clowns.

Lucy had been expertly avoiding them, keeping her distance from people, sticking to the lanes and back-alleys, and ensuring she was never far from something to duck down behind. Gymnastics class didn't include hedge vaulting, but if it had, Lucy would have been top of the class.

It helped that the clowns didn't seem to be very observant. They seemed to be focused on the people they were with. They watched, they whispered, they nudged and prodded, pushed and pulled. Lucy had seen mind control before, even experienced it herself.

This was something else.

She'd seen a clown stop a child from stepping out into the road. A split second later and the kid would have been in the path of a car on the school run.

What did you do about invisible invaders that saved kids from being run over? Lucy didn't know, but staying out of their way was where she was going to start.

Which, when she turned around, made the clown

standing behind her... inconvenient.

CHAPTER SIXTEEN

A CAST OF NOBODIES

Harlequin had found some boxes and had them arranged to make a small raised stage in the middle of the Big Top. It was far from the grandeur and spectacle that he was used to, but a stage was a stage, even if there wasn't much of an audience.

What was left of his troupe was assembled before him. It seemed that the box, the big blue box was supposed to have disposed of the girl, did not like to be tampered with. It had backfired. It had backfired and eaten his glorious, precious, irreplaceable clowns.

It hadn't eaten them whole. But it had consumed some vital part of them, leaving them less than they had been before. They were banana skins, apple cores, the crusts of toast left on the plate… They were reduced, made small, made insignificant. Harlequin could endure many things, *had* endured many things, but insignificance was not one of them.

A few Pantalones shifted and fidgeted anxiously. A less observant creature might have simply assumed they were afraid, but Harlequin was an expert, a connoisseur of fear, and he knew when people were afraid of him and when they were afraid of something – or someone – else. The Pantalones weren't their usual selves. They had fled the circus with the humans, followed them like lapdogs. They no longer performed; they served.

The Dotore, once the engineers and geniuses of the troupe, were now little more than the old and doddering men that they had pretended to be. Harlequin had relished the Dotore for their hidden brilliance, their minds like sharks lurking just below the water. But no more.

'Is this it?' Harlequin hissed to his ever-so faithful companion, Art, who was lurking at the foot of the stage.

'We have the Brighella, your lordship,' replied Art. 'They are caged now, for safety.'

Harlequin nodded. He was no stranger to savagery and violence, but his was the kind of savagery that came draped in silks and smelling of the finest perfumes. He considered it a luxury to descend into blood-red rage. The Brighella were enjoying no such luxury. The Patalone had become servants, the Dotore fools, and the Brighella were now savages: brutal, cruel, and monstrous. They had no minds, only instincts – the instincts to hunt, to eat, and to kill.

'Keep them caged,' said Harlequin. 'But not fed. They need to be hungry.'

At least, Harlequin thought. *I know how to use a monster.*

CHAPTER SEVENTEEN

BEFORE YOUR VERY EYES

Lucy froze. Her PE teacher, Mr Barrett, was standing right in front of her, and so was his clown. Lucy remembered the type – Pierrot, the sad one with the buttons.

She stared at it.

It stared at her.

It smiled.

Mr Barrett smiled.

When the thing spoke, though only in a whisper, very softly into Mr Barret's ear, Lucy could somehow still tell what it was saying. Its voice, she realised, was just like hers had become. You couldn't hear it, but that didn't mean people didn't listen.

'The children will enjoy their trip,' whispered the clown. 'You and Mr Grant have done good work.'

'They'll enjoy that,' said Mr Barrett to himself. 'Not a bad job, if I say so myself.'

The clown nodded, and Lucy watched as it

patted Mr Barrett on the shoulder and the pair turned to leave.

'Hang on a minute!' blurted Lucy. 'Can you see me or what?'

Both clown and teacher turned back to face her.

'Now,' said Mr Barrett, 'did I see Lucy Wilson on that bus?'

The Pierrot looked at Lucy, its face twisted with confusion. It looked like a dog which had suddenly been asked to solve an equation.

It whispered to Mr Barrett again.

'Yes, of course I did,' he said to himself. 'Where else would she be?'

He turned once more and headed through the school gates, muttering to himself as he went, 'Come on, Dennis, you old clown, you've got work to do.'

Lucy watched as Mr Barrett and Dennis the clown headed across the playground towards the main building. She was pretty certain that Mr Barrett had actually been referring to himself as Dennis, but somehow the clown seemed less sinister if he had a name. She let them get a little way ahead before she started to follow them.

She needed to know where the school trip was headed, and to work out just how invisible she was. The clown had seen her, but it had barely reacted to her at all. It had seemed more confused than anything.

Lucy caught a glimpse of herself reflected in a window. She was startled for a second, before she remembered that she had woken up this morning with a full face of circus clown make-up. She was glad that in her confusion she hadn't thought of washing it off, because now it felt like camouflage. Ever since she had moved to Ogmore, school had felt like enemy territory. Now she was about to go behind enemy lines.

She followed Mr Barrett through the front doors and into the main corridor. The first thing she noticed was how clean everything was. There was a smell of fresh paint in the air, and walls that had the day before been pock-marked and pitted and stained with damp were now pristine white. New signs pointed to places Lucy was certain had never existed there before: 'Maths Ball Pit', 'History Foam Slide', and 'Geography Merry-Go-Round'.

Dennis the Clown nudged Mr Barrett to turn left, towards the staff room, and Lucy hurried to keep up. As they passed Lucy's hated Wall of Achievement, she realised that educational soft-play mash-ups weren't the only improvements to the school. Eighteen inches across, framed in gold, was a picture of Hobo.

'G. Kostinen. Outstanding Academic Achievement.'

'G' Kostinen? Was that Hobo? Lucy had known

him that long and still she hadn't asked his real name. She smiled. 'Good for you, Hobo.' For alien invaders, the clowns seemed to be getting some things right, it seemed.

The clunk of a door closing made Lucy realise she'd lost track of Mr Barrett and Dennis, the two of them vanishing into the hallowed ground of the staff room. Lucy crept up to the door and pressed her ear against it. She waited, straining to hear any useful titbit of information. Then it occurred to her that she might as well be invisible.

'Head in the game, Lethbridge-Stewart,' she muttered to herself, and she carefully pushed the door open and slipped inside.

On the other side of the door, Lucy found most of the teachers sitting around chatting, the radio playing quietly in the background.

There were other clowns there too: some Dotoroes, two Pantalones and one Lucy didn't recognise. She wondered if there was something important about the type of clown that you got.

She remembered that Grandad had described some aliens to her once – one was the Daleks, squid-like creatures in war machines, with no other goal but to exterminate anything that wasn't like them; another were the Cybermen, men who had enhanced themselves with artificial limbs and removed all emotion, and wanted everybody else to be like them, too. All aliens ever seemed to want to do was kill or convert anything that wasn't the same as them. Lucy's grandad had said that humanity's greatest strength was that everyone was different. Maybe that was what drew the aliens here. Maybe everywhere else in the universe things were the same, and only on Earth everything was different.

Well, if getting rid of different things was what they wanted, they were off to a good start. Lucy had been the most different girl in town, and now nobody seemed to notice that she was there.

Lucy sidled up to one of the other teachers. She still had no idea why the clowns were ignoring her, but she didn't want to test her luck with Dennis again. She did have a test in mind though.

'I wonder when the kids will be back from wherever they are...'

Lucy held her breath. None of the clowns reacted, only carried on fussing with their respective humans, but Mrs Harris from the Art Department looked suddenly curious.

'I wonder when the kids will be back,' he said wistfully. 'From wherever they are...'

'Won't take them long to get down to the sea front,' replied another of the PE teachers, Mr Harding. 'Puppet show can't last that long. Reckon we've got time for one more cup of tea?'

The other teachers chuckled. Someone put the

kettle on.

Lucy grinned. Invisible and in the staff room, controlling the minds of her teachers... She was pretty sure she had had a dream like this once, just with fewer clowns.

— CHAPTER EIGHTEEN —
ONE WOBBLY WHEEL

Harlequin pushed the trolley slowly up aisle nine. Jams and preserves to his left, baking accessories to his right. The trolley must have had a wobbly wheel. Or perhaps he was contesting for control of it with some unseen and unknowable force. Harlequin couldn't be sure; he'd never been to the supermarket before.

'This is where they come?' he asked Art, who was trailing behind him with his own trolley. 'When they want food?'

'It is where they come for supplies of all sorts, my lord.'

'Supplies.' Harlequin hissed the word as if it might burn out his tongue. 'But where are the vendors? Where are the artisans?'

'They use machines to make their food,' replied Art. 'They call it mass production.'

Harlequin spat onto the floor. The fish and chips had been bad enough, but this... this was intolerable.

Art turned left at the end of the aisle and

Harlequin followed.

'We've been here,' said Harlequin with a hiss. 'I recognise that creature on the pot of… what was it called?'

'Yoghurt, my lord.'

'Yes, yog… hurt.'

Art turned again, this time into an aisle that was mysteriously chilly. Stark and white, its shelves were lined with packages of raw meat.

'At last,' said Art with a sigh, as he began to load packet after packet into his trolley.

Harlequin picked up a packet and placed it on the floor.

'It does not even flee,' he said, marvelling at the two pork chops sitting motionless in their plastic tray. 'This is no kind of hunt.'

Art sighed and placed the pork chops in the trolley.

'How much longer will this take, Art? I hold out little hope, but I would like to at least see the unexpected items in what they call the bagging area.'

'They sound divine, my lord, but if we are to survive on this world we are going to need to learn its customs.'

'I did not come here to survive,' spat Harlequin. 'I came here to conquer. I came here to steal a world away from that idiot Pierrot and make Columbine my own. I do not understand why this world is so important.'

'Look around you, my lord. See the humans, really see them. See the servants. See the fools. See the lovestruck teenagers. See the brigands and the thieves. Can you not see the clowns in them all? There is a reason that Pierrot wants this place for Columbine. I believe that this planet, this Earth, is where we were born.'

Harlequin shot a look at Art. 'We weren't supposed to return here,' he said. 'They say that this planet is protected by the many-faced clown.'

'Do you think,' asked Harlequin tentatively, 'that the girl is…?'

'Important?'

'Possibly.' Harlequin murmured. He was thinking. Something shifted in the air, as if the universe itself was trying to squirm away from whatever it was that he had in mind. When finally he did move, it was only to laugh. Laugh and laugh and laugh.

'I am so glad that I made you, my darling,' he said, patting Art on the head. 'I made you both wise and useful.'

Harlequin gave an exuberant twirl, tossing another handful of surprisingly compliant meat in the trolley. Art threw the long spaghetti he had been manhandling alongside it. 'Spaghetti Bolognese,' he said. 'A human delicacy.'

'Pierrot thinks me trapped, Art,' said Harlequin. 'He knew I would come here to steal this world from him. Knew that I would reach out to my allies, that I would spoil his plans for a gift to sweet, sweet Columbine.'

'And yet are we not trapped, my lord?' asked Art.

'Far from it,' replied Harlequin. 'We are never trapped. We are clown. It is our very art to escape the inescapable. And when we escape, and we will escape, this whole word will cheer.'

'What would you have me do, sir?'

'We return to the circus,' commanded Harlequin. 'And we release the Brighella.'

— CHAPTER NINETEEN —

THAT'S THE WAY TO DO IT

The school bus pulled into the small car park on the edge of the beach. Hobo stared out of the window. Not-Lucy wasn't much of a conversationalist; mostly she just repeated what was said to her. The other kids didn't seem to notice. They didn't seem to notice anything that was different.

'Things are good. The other children all like you; they all want to be your friend. Lucy is popular. You are popular. School is a fun place to be.'

Hobo closed his eyes and tried to block out the whispering. It had stopped for a while, drowned out by the noise of the other kids, but since they'd left school and begun their journey down to the seaside, the whole bus had been eerily quiet. The cheering had stopped, the chatter had stopped, and the other kids were all silent, lost in their own internal worlds.

'You all hear the whispering too, don't you?'

mused Hobo to himself, opening his eyes and looking suspiciously around at the other children.

'Yes, I hear the whispering,' replied Not-Lucy.

'Not you.'

At the front of the bus, the door hissed open, and the children stood up in unison and began to disembark. Normally it would have been a crush, a stampede, but not today. Today the children filed off one at a time, and everyone remembered to thank the driver.

Hobo closed his eyes again for a moment as he waited for his turn.

'Guard your mind, guard your mind, guard your mind,' he repeated to himself. He had no idea if this would be enough, but it had worked with the Great Intelligence, and it was the only thing that he could think to do. He wished Lucy was here, the real Lucy.

Not-Lucy stood and joined the queue, and Hobo followed. Nobody pushed past, nobody jeered at Hobo to hurry up. They just waited, patient, polite and creepily silent.

'Sorry,' muttered Hobo, grabbing his school bag and shuffling off the bus.

Things were no less weird outside. The same quiet and orderly line of children was filing its way silently to the Punch and Judy show. One by one, the other kids arranged themselves in neat, cross-legged rows in front of the old wooden box. There were other people there too, all waiting for the show.

Hobo felt a tremor of fear as he approached at the box. Something from his dream – not exactly the same but close enough to resonate; something that made him scared of the box and whatever was inside of it. He wanted to break away from the other kids and find himself somewhere to sit as far away from the Punch and Judy box as possible.

'There is nothing to be afraid of. This is the greatest show in the universe.'

'That's not reassuring,' Hobo whispered back to whoever his invisible companion was. 'And besides, I've seen it.'

Some of the children who had been quietly walking in line behind Hobo overtook him, railroading him into a spot where he had no choice but to sit down. It wasn't as near the front as it could have been, but it was still closer than he was comfortable with.

Inside the Punch and Judy box, Pete watched the crowd through a small, hidden peep-hole. Children had been arriving since early morning. Pete had liked it better when nobody came to hear his stories.

This was Harlequin's doing, he was sure of it. But Harlequin had made a mistake, the same mistake he always made. He always assumed he was the clever one, the cunning one, the smart one. He always thought that he was the only one with a plan.

But Pete had a plan of his own.

Lucy's lungs were on fire by the time she caught up with the bus. *I may be invisible,* she thought. *But my legs are definitely real. Very real, and very tired.*

'Mental note,' she said with a wheeze, 'buy a bike.'

The school bus was letting off the last of her school mates. She watched, concealed behind a bus stop, as the clowns herded them along in orderly lines. They were careful, gentle, and Lucy wondered if anyone else had any idea the clowns were there at all.

Of course, if there was one person that could be relied on to beat mysterious circus-themed alien mind control, it was Hobo. Lucy picked out his bulky frame and bald head from the crowd, and her heart soared when she saw him break from the line. His clown, a Dotore with a long beard, shuffled after him, and others guided their children to hem him in. Lucy's fingers closed around the radio in her pocket, but she didn't dare to use it. Hobo was surrounded, and he didn't even know it.

'Lethbridge-Stewart time it is then,' Lucy said to herself. 'A daring rescue behind enemy lines, outnumbered and outgunned.'

Stepping out from behind the bus stop, she

dashed across the road, taking up a new vantage point behind the school bus.

Pete looked out from inside his box. The boy was here, his bald head and wide shoulders unmistakable amongst the crowd. The girl was here too, lurking behind the school bus. And the other, the duplicate that Harlequin's machine had made.

Pete had recognised the machine the moment he saw it. It was from the deepest, darkest parts of their history. It was sacred. It was feared. It was ancient and powerful, and Harlequin had found it, somehow, and brought it there to deal with one little girl.

Pete crouched down in his tiny wooden box and opened up his old suitcase. Underneath the normal puppets – Mr Punch, Mrs Punch, the crocodile, the policeman – there was a sheet of old newspaper. Pete pulled it to one side. Underneath the newspaper were other puppets, older puppets that Pete had brought with him when he first came here. There was Harlequin, Colombine, Pierrot, and all of the other clowns – perfect replicas for him to play out his story. There were other puppets too: a man, hairy and wearing nothing but an animal skin; another man in old fashioned clothes with a wild expression and staring eyes. Last, but not possibly least, was the clown with many faces.

He was Pete's favourite puppet. He had been made on a planet very, very far away, carved from wood taken from forests that sang when it rained and told secrets when the wind blew just right. All wood was alive before it was chopped down and carved into new and interesting shapes, but only very special wood remained alive afterwards. The puppet of the clown with many faces never looked the same for long. It was always changing, which was how it would last forever.

But the first character of this story wasn't the many-faced clown. It was Pete himself. Slowly, he raised his puppet into the view of the crowd.

'Ladies and gentlemen, children of all ages, what you are about to see is the oldest and most important story that I know. It is a story that I have brought with me from a place far, far away. It is the story of how clowns came to be.'

There were gasps in the crowd and spontaneous flutters of applause.

'In the beginning, there is only man.'

Pete raised his caveman puppet. It began to snuffle around the stage, banging its club on the ground.

'Man looks at himself. Says… what am I?' Pete's clown puppet crept up behind the caveman and tapped it on the shoulder. The caveman turned, the clown dodging behind him before he was seen. 'And clown is born. Clown is invisible, but man hears his whispers. Clown wants what is good for man.'

Pete expertly operated the puppets, miming the clown directing the caveman around the stage. 'But man is fickle. Man is violent. Man is capricious and cruel. Clown begins to become like man, whispers only dark things in man's ear. Dark things lead to dark deeds. Clown makes man laugh and laugh and laugh and laugh.'

The crowd began to laugh. Quietly at first, then louder and louder, until they were laughing so hard that they couldn't catch their breath.

Pete replaced the caveman with another wild-eyed clown from his box. In the crowd, laughter had turned into gasping and choking. With a click of his fingers, Pete released them from his spell. He had forgotten how it felt to hold an audience in the palm of his hand. He wanted to clutch them to his chest and hold them there forever. But he had work to do.

'That was when he came. Man's protector, the clown with many faces. The ancient one with the heart of a child..'

Pete raised his final puppet, the strange-looking puppet with the face that changed. Between his tiny wooden hands he held a mirror on the end of a long stick.

'He came and tricked them into seeing their own face. He showed them what they had become.'

The wild-eyed clown disappeared out of sight, leaving only the clown and the stranger.

'Man was free from clown. Clown was free from man and promised never to return to Earth. We began our new life among the stars, leaving only stories behind. Man still laughs when he sees clown, but he never truly knows why.'

The crowd broke into rapturous applause. Pete, peeping out of his box, watched as people and their clowns wiped tears from their eyes. Sadness and joy, the cornerstones of the shared history of men and clown. Sadness and joy created by Pete and his puppets.

'Now,' Pete whispered to himself inside his box, 'real show begins.'

— CHAPTER TWENTY —

AUDIENCE PARTICIPATION

Lucy crept through the crowd, closing in on Hobo. Everyone, including the clowns, was so enraptured by the puppet show that, even if Lucy hadn't known she was invisible, she would have felt confident in her gambit. Easing her way between her classmates, she realised that she actually didn't have a clue what to do next. Lucy ran on gut instinct most of the time; Hobo was the thinker, the one who made plans.

Right behind him now, she leant forwards and whispered, 'Hobo, can you hear me?'

Hobo's back stiffened. Gingerly, he unhooked his rucksack from over his shoulder, opened it slowly and reached deep inside. Looking furtively left and right, he pulled out the broken parts of what must have once been his radio.

'Not on the radio, Hobo. I'm here. I'm with you!'

Hobo shoved the broken radio back into his

rucksack.

'I don't know who you are, but leave me alone,' he whispered. 'I'm not listening to you.'

Hobo looked around again. Her doppelganger was there, sitting with a group of girls that Lucy would never normally hang around with. She was smiling. She was laughing. Lucy hated her. She could feel her temper boiling up inside her.

'That's not me, Hobo! I'm not a dummy! I'm not a clown. I'm Lucy. *Lucy!*'

Hobo turned, slowly, but his eyes looked right through her.

'Do you hear me, Hobo?' she shouted, waving her hands in front of his face. 'It's me. I'm not a clown! I'm Lucy! Lucy!'

'You're Lucy…'

Lucy looked to her side. A clown, one of the Pierrots, with its white and black outfit and tearful face, was looking at her. Right at her.

'You're Lucy…'

Behind her, another clown, a Pantalone, staring. Pointing.

'Oh no,' said Lucy. 'Hobo, if you've been holding out on me, now would be a really, really good time to do something.'

But Hobo didn't answer, just stared stonily ahead as one by one the clowns turned to point at her.

'You're Lucy.'

'You're not clown.'

'You're Lucy.'

'You're not clown.'

'Lucy.'

'Not clown.'

'Lucy.'

'Lucy.'

'Lucy.'

As one, the clowns started to move towards Lucy. Slowly at first, carefully creeping around the people they had brought with them, but gradually building up speed. They reached out, their long-fingered hands grasping at the air as they approached her.

'OK, Hobo,' said Lucy. 'We're out of here whether you like it or not!'

Spotting a gap, Lucy grabbed Hobo's hand and made a break through the crowd. He was heavy, but in his surprise he was soon moving, tripping over his own feet but following. Unlike the clowns, Lucy didn't care who she and Hobo collided with. They crashed through the first row of kids, then the second, heading away from the road and towards the beach.

People were screaming, terrified as the invisible force of Lucy, and the very visible force of Hobo, trampled over them. Then Hobo dug his heels in, bringing them to a stop.

'What are you doing to me?' he shouted. 'Let me

go!'

Lucy kept hold of his hand and pulled again, heaving with all her might to try and get him moving.

'I'm trying to save you!'

'Let me go!' shouted Hobo, yanking his hand free.

A clown grabbed him from behind and pulled him away.

'No!' screamed Lucy, 'Leave him alone!'

Suddenly, Lucy was spun around by a strong hand on her shoulder. The old man who ran the Punch and Judy show was behind her.

'They not listen to you,' he said flatly. 'Run. Get in box.'

He pointed to the Punch and Judy show behind him.

'You can see me?' Lucy asked incredulously.

'Of course,' the man replied. 'I am clown. Now get in box.'

Lucy pulled away from the old man. The clowns were getting closer on all sides. Hobo was held fast, struggling against forces that Lucy knew he couldn't see. More people were screaming. Up on the road, cars were stopping and people getting out. People with clowns.

Lucy looked at the box. 'No way,' she said. 'Not again. And not without Hobo.'

The old man looked at her sourly.

'Fine,' he replied. 'I get boy. You get in box. Is deal.'

Without another word, the old man ploughed forwards, hurling the two nearest clowns away from him with impossible strength. They crashed into two other clowns, bowling them over. Lucy watched as he wrestled Hobo free from the clown that was holding him, shoving the clown to the ground.

'Wow!' said Lucy.

'Box!' grunted the old man. Shoving Lucy ahead and towing Hobo behind him, he strode back towards the little Punch and Judy show, tossing another clown through the air when it got too close.

'Inside.'

Hobo was pushed in first, followed by Lucy. Turning to face the approaching clowns, Pete threw the little wooden door closed behind them. Hobo was breathing hard, sweat beading his face. He looked terrified. He *was* terrified.

'Hobo,' said Lucy gently. 'I'm so sorry.'

In the darkness inside the box, Lucy saw something glinting. In the old man's suitcase, where he kept his puppets, was a little mirror on a stick, the same one she had seen him use in the show. She could see herself in it. Her clown make-up was streaked, her own darker skin showing through in places, her red nose smudged away.

He showed them their true face, she thought,

remembering a part of the old man's story. *He is a clown too, he said as much. A clown that everyone could see.*

Lucy reached down and picked up the mirror. She angled it so that she could see Hobo's face. She waited. In the gloom, she watched as Hobo's eyes adjusted, as if he'd just taken off a pair of strong spectacles.

He reached out a trembling hand, his fingers gently touching her cheek.

'Lucy?' he said, his voice trembling. 'Is that you?'

Lucy smiled. 'Yes, Hobo, it's me. It's Lucy.'

Hobo lunged forwards, wrapping his arms around her. She hugged him back, forgetting for a moment everything that was going on outside, even as the sides of the Punch and Judy box rocked back and forth around them. It didn't matter. They were back together. The team was back together.

Lucy Lethbridge-Stewart and Hobo Kostinen, the scourge of aliens everywhere.

Especially Ogmore-by-Sea.

— CHAPTER TWENTY-ONE —

NOT A MAGIC BOX

Pete wrenched open the small door of the Punch and Judy box and forced his way inside, crushing Lucy and Hobo up against the flimsy walls, before pulling the small door closed behind him.

'Breathe in,' he said.

'Not much choice,' said Hobo. 'This thing is smaller than it looks.'

Pete looked sideways at Hobo. 'What you expect? Is not magic box.'

Pushing up against Lucy and Hobo, Pete dug his fingers into one wall, pulling away a panel. Lucy and Hobo could see wiring, lights, switches and old fashioned push buttons.

'Is spaceship,' muttered Pete grumpily.

Hobo and Lucy watched, mouths hanging open, as the old man flipped switches and pushed buttons.

'Is old spaceship,' said Pete, correcting himself. 'So breathe in. Hold breath.'

Outside the Punch and Judy box, people stood and

watched as it stopped rocking from side to side, propelled by the unseen hands of the invisible clowns, and collapsed in on itself. It folded down quite neatly, like a castle in a pop-up book, and then it was gone.

The only possible response was to applaud.

'Fair play,' someone said loudly, 'he's really raised his game since the circus came to town'.

Gasping for air, Lucy and Hobo tumbled out of the box into a dark, quiet place. Pete stepped over them.

'Told you,' he said with a grunt. 'Hold breath.'

Untangling themselves from each other, Lucy and Hobo got awkwardly to their feet. They looked around, their eyes adjusting to the gloom. Above them, suspended in the darkness, they could see puppets. Clown puppets, people puppets, animal puppets, and puppets of things so strange and monstrous that neither Lucy nor Hobo could bear to look at them for long.

The rest of the place, as best they could see, was crammed with mirrors, tables, boxes, and make-shift work surfaces piled high with fragments of puppets that had not yet been completed.

'Where are we?' whispered Hobo.

'My home,' replied Pete, shuffling around somewhere in the gloom.

'Who on earth are you?' asked Hobo.

'On Earth?' Pete chuckled. 'Strange question. On Earth, I am Pete. I am the Punch and Judy man. Puppet man, in box. That is on Earth.'

'And before?' asked Lucy. 'Before you came to Earth?'

Pete smiled, his lined and wrinkled face creasing into new contours.

'Before? Before I was Lord Punchinella, of House Punchinella. I was clown.'

'A clown?' said Hobo.

'No, not "a" clown. I was clown. Like…'

Pete reached out and put his hand on Hobo's chest.

'You… Human. I… Clown. Punchinella the Clown.'

'Clowns are aliens?' asked Hobo incredulously.

'I told you!' whispered Lucy. 'Are we on another planet, Punchinella?'

'No,' replied Punchinella gruffly. 'Is bungalow.'

He threw open some curtains, filling the room with light and revealing the unmistakable vista of Ogmore-by-Sea.

Hobo let out a sigh of relief. 'Thank goodness! I don't think I've ever been so pleased to see Ogmore!'

'Speak for yourself,' grumbled Lucy.

Hobo turned to look at Lucy. Still in her going out clothes, her face painted white, the tip of her nose bright red. In the mirrors that surrounded them, Lucy looked at herself too.

'I hate to say it, but that other you is definitely better at putting on make-up,' said Hobo.

'Ha ha,' said Lucy sarcastically. 'Remind me again why I rescued you?'

'Maybe after you tell me what exactly you rescued me from.'

Any answer Lucy might have given was drowned out by a sudden crash as Punchinella swept a tabletop clear of tools and half-constructed puppets.

'They are clown,' the old man said over his shoulder, 'and I rescued you. Both of you.'

Hobo and Lucy exchanged awkward looks. This wasn't the first time they'd been rescued by a mysterious stranger.

Tossing a pile of old newspapers aside, Punchinella put a chair down in front of the table.

'Sit,' ordered Punchinella, pointing at Lucy and then at the chair. 'I fix face.'

'I just want to wash it off,' said Lucy. 'Don't you have a bathroom?'

'Sit,' repeated Punchinella firmly. 'I fix.'

'Do as the crazy puppet man says, Lucy,' said Hobo. 'I think he is on our side.'

'You're sure?'

Hobo nodded. 'Actually, yeah. Don't ask me why.'

'Met before,' said Punchinella, pointing at Hobo.

'I don't remember.'

'You will.'

— CHAPTER TWENTY-ONE —

THE LAUGHTER HUNT

'What do you mean he disappeared?!' screeched Harlequin. The Pantalone delivering the report shuffled its feet. At Harlequin's side, Art waited impatiently. Some people had a short fuse, but right now Harlequin had no fuse at all. He was a fireball of rage, and the whole circus was caught in the blast.

'Answer,' said Art coldly. 'Please.'

'The box, my lord. It vanished. It gone. It just… folded up.'

The Pantalone winced, shutting its eyes tight.

'The Folding Space,' said Harlequin, a smile of razor teeth splitting his alabaster-white face. 'Oh you old fool, Punchinella!'

Harlequin dipped his head and placed a kiss on the nose of the terrified Pantalone.

'You can go, my darling,' he said sweetly.

'You have a plan, my lord?' asked Art.

'Only the Lords of the Great Clown Houses know the Folding Space and its limitations…'

Art waited for Harlequin to complete his ominous pause. Every moment was a performance with Harlequin. In Art's opinion it just slowed things down.

'The Folding Space links the Great Houses of Clown across the universe. It is how I move this troupe and this circus. It allows us to visit each other, to take our performance to any part of time and space.'

'So he could be anywhere,' Art said. 'Anywhere in space and time?'

'Oh no,' replied Harlequin, licking his dark lips. 'He is near. He is the last of House Punchinella, and this mudball world is his family seat. He will not have abandoned it.'

Harlequin was building up to something, Art could tell.

'The Folding Space can never be used in secret, my lovely Art,' he explained finally. 'It was built for performers, for diplomats, and for royalty. Despite his diminished status, Lord Punchinella is still all three of those things. The Folding Space will have *announced* him, Art. It has to.'

There was reason that the Folding Space announced the arrival of clowns.

It wasn't to fill seats in a Big Top.

It was a warning.

*

Punchinella stared at Lucy, his nose almost touching her eyeball.

'I've taken make-up off before,' she grumbled. 'Do you have any cotton wool or—?'

'Is not make-up,' replied Punchinella. 'Is clown. Clown face, on your face. You think clowns so stupid they think girl in make-up is clown?'

Lucy looked sideways at Hobo. He just shrugged. 'It does seem unlikely.'

'Fine,' said Lucy. 'So, how do we get it off?'

Punchinella shuffled off and started yanking at drawers and flipping open the lids of chests and boxes.

'We bring back true face,' he muttered. 'Obvious.'

'My true face?'

Lucy looked at herself in the mirror. Wasn't this her? Sure, there was the white greasepaint, but she could still see herself underneath it.

Punchinella unscrewed the lid of a dirty old jar.

'Here,' he said, dumping the jar down on the dressing table in front of Lucy. 'For clown face.'

Gently he pushed Lucy's head forwards, so that she was looking down into it. As she got closer, she could feel something pulling on her face, some invisible force from inside the jar. She winced, screwing up her eyes.

'You're hurting her!' said Hobo, reaching out to pull Punchinella's hand from the back of Lucy's head.

'Pain is only way,' said the old man firmly, using his spare hand to hold Hobo at bay.

'It's… OK, Hobo,' Lucy gasped. The pain was building now; it felt tiny pins pricks all across her face – invisible needles poking and, somehow, unstitching.

Punchinella leaned forwards, his mouth close to Lucy's ear.

'Doing well. Brave,' he said quietly. 'Now tell me name of house.'

'House?' asked Lucy.

'Your house,' insisted Punchinella. 'Name your house.'

'I live at number—'

'No, no!' interrupted the old man. 'Your house. Name your house!'

'I think he means your surname, Lucy,' said Hobo. 'Like in history class, the name of your house, right? Your family name.'

'Wilson,' said Lucy. 'My house is Wilson.'

Suddenly, the pain in Lucy's face flared and she let out a cry.

'What's happening?' yelled Hobo.

'Is not working,' replied Punchinella. 'Name of house not working.'

Lucy let out another cry. Her face felt like it was on fire, her features melting under the heat of the make-up.

'What does that mean?' asked Hobo.

'Clown face become face. No more girl… only clown.'

Punchinella let go of Lucy and began to pace around the cramped room.

Hobo pushed past him, grabbing hold of Lucy by the shoulders. He could feel her shaking in his grasp, the pain convulsing through her body.

'Lucy, it's me. It's Hobo.'

Lucy gave a gasp, then another cry. She brought her hands, trembling, up to her face. Hobo watched as, inch by inch, Lucy's normal skin was replaced by the white, greasy flesh of the clown. Her hair, from the roots towards the tip, was slowly turning bright green, and the tip of her nose had started to grow and grow.

'Don't try to speak,' said Hobo, his own voice weak. 'We're going to figure this out.'

Behind him, Hobo could hear Punchinella pacing and muttering to himself.

'How does this work?' snapped Hobo, keeping his eyes on Lucy in the mirror, watching as she was slowly consumed by clown.

'Open jar. Give true name. Clown face in jar, simple,' muttered the old man. 'Jar may be broken. Is very old. Very old.'

'True name,' Hobo said to himself. 'True name… That's it!'

Hobo tightened his grip on Lucy. He was sure he was right. He *had* to be right.

'Lucy, you didn't give the true name of your house,' he said, keeping his voice as calm as he could.

In the mirror, he could see Lucy's features slowly distorting: her nose growing elongated, her mouth twisting into a maniacal grin. Two red circles had appeared on her cheeks, blossoming against the pure white.

'I know I've been cross with you about it,' Hobo continued, 'but it's really important now. Really, really important. I need you to tell me who you are. Who you really are. Do you understand?'

Lucy nodded. 'It hurts, Hobo.'

'I know,' said Hobo, forcing himself to ignore the fact that Lucy hardly sounded like Lucy anymore, forcing himself to ignore the changes in her face, forcing himself to ignore everything except the thought of saving his best friend.

'Who are you?' he asked.

For a second, maybe two, there was no answer. The clown who had been Lucy opened its eyes and looked at itself in the mirror. It saw its face, a pure and brilliant white now, with its long nose and twisted smile. It saw its hair, a frizzy mane of green. It turned left and right, examining itself in the mirror. Hobo realised that he was watching a creature seeing itself for the very first time, a new creature just born into the world.

'Who are you?' he asked again, his voice little more than a whisper.

'I'm… I'm…'

The creature could not answer. The clown that had been Lucy stared at itself again, and this time, in the mirror, Hobo realised that he could see something else. Right there, staring back at him. The one thing that hadn't changed. Hobo was looking right into Lucy's eyes.

The clown that had been Lucy smiled and spoke. 'I'm Lucy,' it said. 'Lucy Lethbridge-Stewart.'

Suddenly the mirror shattered, spraying glass across the room. Hobo ducked reflexively, pulling Lucy down towards the ground with him. She was hot to the touch. It was like accidentally touching the oven door when dinner was being prepared.

'The jar!' shouted Punchinella. 'The jar!'

Hobo scrambled to his feet and retrieved the jar from the dressing table. Punchinella snatched it out of his hands and, dropping down to the ground, levered Lucy upright, placing her head over it. She groaned, the long and low groans of someone trying to wake from a nightmare, her head lolling to one side as Punchinella held her up.

'Lethbridge-Stewart,' the old man said quietly to himself. 'This house is known.'

Hobo watched as Lucy's face, her clown face, slowly slithered off. It came away like the skin of a lizard, whole and intact. It writhed and squirmed, flopping like a fish pulled from the water. Punchinella moved Lucy back and forth to skillfully pour the thing into the jar. Hobo watched with a grim fascination as the empty, eyeless face pressed itself against the inside of the glass, its mouth open in a silent scream.

Finally, when the last of the thing had peeled itself away from Lucy, Punchinella slammed the lid into place and screwed it down tight. Lucy lay on the floor, barely breathing. Hobo reached out a hand, gingerly, towards her.

Punchinella looked at him.

'Is safe now,' he said flatly. 'Care for friend.'

Hobo crawled over to Lucy, pulling off his hoodie and bundling it up into a makeshift pillow. He lifted her gently and laid her down in a more comfortable position. He smiled at the sight of her, the real her, once again. He didn't dare to think about how close he had come to losing her.

— CHAPTER TWENTY-TWO —
RIDING THE CLOWN

The post office in Ogmore-by-Sea had lots of posters and cards in the window. Two local window cleaners each claimed to be Ogmore's 'original' window cleaner, a plumber offered quick call outs, and half the town seemed to be offering their bikes for sale.

There was also a poster announcing the arrival of a 'Lord Punchinella', making his debut appearance in an Ogmore that day. It was this one that had captured the attention of Harlequin.

He had ridden into the town on the back of a Brighella. The power of the magic box had reduced them to little more than animals, but they still had their uses. Harlequin had asked the Dotore to fashion him a saddle. Riding on the back, the largest of them, a clown almost seven feet tall and with a chest like the bonnet of a small car, wasn't the most comfortable way to travel, but there wasn't a single creature in the galaxy that didn't enjoy a piggy-back, not even Harlequin. And fun had been in rather short supply since his disastrous attempt to expunge Lucy Wilson from this world.

Ideally, he needed to kill something. For now, a piggy-back would do.

Harlequin had known it would be posted somewhere. No Lord of Clowns could be using the Folding Space without his arrival being notified.

It was etiquette.

It was the rules.

Lucy stared at her tea cup, suspecting, just a little, that it might be staring back. She'd never had tea made by an alien before. There could be anything in it.

Hobo seemed to have acclimatised to things though. He was on to his third cup and had his eye on a second piece of cake. Lucy stole a glance at herself in one of the mirrors that were hanging from the walls. Everything was back to normal. Yet something still seemed wrong to her. Something felt missing. She just couldn't put her finger on what.

'This is nice,' she said, taking a polite sip of tea. 'But I think it's time for us to talk.'

The old man put his cup down.

'Talk.'

'Like, for example, why is there a clown in my house?' And why are there invisible clowns everywhere else? And who are you? Why did you help us? Why did I even wake up looking like a clown, what was that thing on my face, and how is there some creepy copy of me wandering around town after stealing my breakfast?'

It was the most Lucy had said since she'd woken up. The words hung in the air like storm clouds, the silence only broken by a tiny piece of glass dropping out of Lucy's hair and shattering on the wooden floor.

Hobo's mouth was hanging open.

'When did all this happen?' he asked numbly.

'You were on the bus.'

'For how long?'

Lucy shrugged.

'Anything else?' asked Punchinella.

'My mum,' replied Lucy, her voice quiet, her temper abating as quickly as it had flared. 'Is she safe?'

Punchinella's face hardened. He pushed Lucy's tea cup towards her.

'Drink.'

'Is she safe?' Lucy persisted.

'No,' Punchinella replied. 'No one safe.'

Lucy looked down at her feet. That same feeling again, as if something was missing. She should have been shouting, raging – doing something at least, but there was nothing. There was a strange emptiness inside her, a sense of disconnection from everything. She was felt like she was pretending to be Lucy. But if she wasn't Lucy, then who was she? She wondered if it was more than just the clown's face that had been stuffed in a jar.

'Why are you here, Punchinella?' she asked. Someone had to ask.

Punchinella looked away, to the one corner of the room where there wasn't a mirror hanging. Instead, in a dusty old frame, under glass, there was a clown's outfit. It wasn't like any of the others that Lucy had seen. It wasn't a Pantalone or a Dotore, but it was unmistakable. A jacket with gaudy red, yellow and blue stripes; a tall black hat flattened down; and a black mask.

'I ran away,' said Punchinella. 'There was a war, and I ran away.'

'What's that?' asked Lucy, pointing at the frame. 'Over there?'

'Is me. Before. Is clothes of Lord Punchinella.'

'So,' said Hobo, 'you're an alien and a lord. Well, you're going to have to forgive us if we don't sound too over the moon about that. We haven't had the best experience with aliens so far.'

Punchinella picked up his cup and drained it, wiping his mouth clean on the back of his hand.

'You want answers. I tell you. Tell you whole story.'

Punchinella got up and, standing on his chair,

began to unhook puppets from the ceiling.

'This is going to be another puppet show, isn't it?' whispered Lucy.

'I'm starting to get the feeling this is how they communicate,' Hobo whispered back. 'Everything's a story with them. A performance.'

They sat in an awkward silence as Punchinella carefully arranged the puppets, sitting them up here and there – on chairs, on boxes, on shelves. Lucy realised that every single one of them was different – a different face, different clothes, different heights and sizes. As creepy as they were, it was impossible for her not to see the love that had gone into their creation.

Placing one last puppet in the chair he had been sitting in, Punchinella began his show.

— CHAPTER TWENTY-THREE —

CIAZARN

Art walked through the circus. The lights were off, the stalls closed, and the Big Top sagged a little. Circus and carnivals had a lot in common with vampires – they only came to life at night. But there was always preparation, always practice. The previous night's rubbish to clean up, tonight's revels to prepare… The stillness, the silence was wrong.

Still, it suited Art's purposes. Harlequin had taken the Brighella on the hunt, the Pantalone were serving their human masters, and the Dotore continued to work on the machine. Art was alone, which was exactly what he needed.

Betrayal was something best done in private.

Art ducked into a tent which promised free palm reading. Inside it was decorated with all the trappings of the fortune teller's trade: some draped-down fabric, a table with a crystal ball, incense and candles burning low. It was amazing how little it took, but it worked the universe over.

Checking the tent flap was closed behind him,

Art took a seat at the table. He didn't need the crystal, but he placed his hands on it all the same. After all, Art was still a clown, and and this was still a performance.

In a low voice, Art began to chant.

'Liazzord Piazzeriot, Hiazzariazzrelquiazzin pliazzots tiazo stiazzealaz Eartiazzth. Liazzord Piazzeriot, Hiazzariazzrelquiazzin hiazzas fiazzailaizzed. Tiaazhe Triaazoupe iaazs fiazzlliazzen.'

Art repeated the message over and over, the soft sound of Ciazarn, the carnival's secret tongue filling the tent. It echoed, impossibly, until the air was filled with it. Like a swarm of invisible insects that burrowed into your ears and filled up your head with their buzzing.

All at once, it stopped. Art's mouth continued to move for a second or two, but there were no more words. There were no more sounds. The secret language of the carnival had been spoken and, across the vast and terrible gulf of space, its message had been heard.

Art stood up, bowed his head for a moment in silent respect, and left the tent.

On a post outside, a poster fluttered in the Ogmore sea breeze.

Art smiled as he read the words emblazoned on it in brightest red and green.

TONIGHT
FOR ONE NIGHT ONLY
THE GREAT PIERROT!
LIVE IN OGMORE-BY-SEA!

'For one night only,' mused Art to himself. 'One night only…'

'Not here, not now, but once, House Punchinella is respected House of Clown.'

Punchinella looked from one puppet to another, then at Lucy and Hobo. They had expected him to move the puppets, to lift them by their strings, but instead they stayed motionless. It was as if he expected them to move on their own.

Punchinella grunted and shrugged. 'War came to House Punchinella. Many die. All die. Except one. I am left. Lord Punchinella. So I run away.' He smudged a tear away from his cheek with his sleeve. 'I come to place no clown should go. I come to Earth.'

'Why does every one of these guys come to Earth?' whispered Hobo.

'Grandad said he knew,' Lucy whispered back. 'Wish he'd told me.'

'You ask, why are clowns here?' said Punchinella, clearly not impressed that his show was being interrupted. 'I already tell you. Clown is born here. Clown from Earth.'

Hobo and Lucy looked at each other, their faces both screwed up with confusion.

'Human look at himself and ask, what am I? To answer question, clown is made. We are the things you are. We are fools. We are scholars. We are warriors. We are cowards. We are leaders. We are servants. You human. We clown. Same but different. You are seen. We are not seen. We are there, but not there.'

Out of the corner of her eye, Lucy thought she saw something move. She jumped, just a little. One of the puppets, a girl with a green dress and golden hair, had slumped forwards. It almost looked like it was listening in on the conversation. Lucy shook her head. That was ridiculous. They were just puppets. Even in a world where school craft projects came to life, or where mobile phones could be possessed by a mysterious force from beyond the stars, Lucy refused to believe in puppets that moved when you weren't looking.

Absolutely, totally, refused to believe.

But she kept her eye on the puppet, just in case.

'This is the story you told at the seaside,' said Hobo. 'What was it... the clown with two faces?'

'Many faces,' corrected Punchinella, smiling. 'Boy pays attention, this is good.'

Hobo smiled despite himself. Lucy wanted to call him a swot, but thought better of it.

'Some say it long time ago,' continued Punchinella. 'Others say not. But time not flat or straight. Sometimes things happen a long time ago, but is still only yesterday. Time misbehave so who can tell? But all know that Clown becomes cruel. Clown want to be man. Clown hurts man and then clown with many faces comes. He not like other Clown. He sees us all.'

'Did he have a name?' asked Lucy. 'This clown who could see the clowns like me?'

'Who knows?' answered Punchinella. 'He is greatest story there is. Oldest story. Always growing. Always changing. Some say his name is what universe whispers to itself before it sleeps, to keep away bad dreams.'

'Lucy, we don't have time to listen to stories,' said Hobo under his breath. 'We need to get our parents out of here.'

'He makes machine,' continued Punchinella, ignoring their conversation. 'Great machine. It cuts clown out of man. Makes clown real. And many-faced clown is kind. He tells clown, go free. Roam. Tell stories to whole universe. Bring laughter. But never come back. Earth is not for Clown.'

'But we have clowns,' said Lucy. 'Mum booked one for my birthday years ago. I didn't like it.'

'You have stories of clowns,' said Punchinella. 'You remember us.'

'You said we'd met before, too,' Hobo said to Punchinella. 'That I would remember you.'

'You will.'

'The machine,' said Lucy. 'It's that box, isn't it, the box that Harlequin put me in?'

'Yes,' replied Pete. 'Harlequin came for you, Lucy Lethbridge-Stewart.'

'Why?' asked Hobo. His voice was hard, even angry. 'Why do they keep coming? The monsters, the aliens, the creatures? What do they want with us?'

Punchinella stopped for a moment. He looked around him, at the puppets. His eyes moved from face to face, as if he might find an answer to the question in their painted-on eyes.

'Greatest House of Clown is House Pierrot,' he began. 'Lord Pierrot loves Lady Columbine, and so does Lord Harlequin. Columbine is most beautiful of all clown, most beloved. All clown stories about her. In our language, Columbine is word for love.'

Lucy scrunched up her face. Love, especially romantic love, wasn't a topic she liked talking about. It was something for dopey romance novels. Grandad and Nanna had been in love up to the end. Connall and Dean were in love, of course, but that was different. They were cute together. But Lucy didn't have time for all that mushy stuff, and the idea of aliens falling in love was definitely something Lucy didn't have time for. That was just… *weird*!

'Pierrot will do anything to win Columbine. Whatever Columbine asks for. And she asks for worlds. Pierrot wants to give her Earth. Harlequin wants to steal it first. Both know girl is one of Earth's defenders.'

'Earth's defenders?' said Lucy. It was one thing to think it, brag to Hobo about it, but it was quite another to say it out loud.

Punchinella put his hand gently on Lucy's shoulder.

'Defender,' he said.

Lucy took a deep breath. Then another. By the third, she was ready.

'Fine,' she said. 'I'm Earth's defender.'

'Lucy,' said Hobo. 'This is big, really big, don't you think—'

'No,' said Lucy, cutting him off. 'I'm Lucy Lethbridge-Stewart, granddaughter of Brigadier Alistair Lethbridge-Stewart. I'm Earth's defender.'

'One of them. There are many,' said Punchinella.

Lucy stood up, pulled herself up to her full height, and looked Punchinella straight in the eyes, her face defiant, his fists clenched by her sides.

'Tell me how to beat him.'

And Punchinella might have had time to tell her, if she hadn't fainted a split second later.

— CHAPTER TWENTY-FOUR —

ANOTHER AFTERNOON
IN OGMORE

Tamara and Albert sat drinking coffee outside Ogmore's only coffee shop. Tamara smiled at Albert. Her memory of the previous night was fuzzy, but she did remember Albert, her knight in shining armour, turning up at the circus and taking her home. And things were better now that he was back in Ogmore, even if his mobile phone wouldn't stop ringing.

'Seventeen missed calls,' he said, holding it up to show Tamara.

'Someone's popular,' she said.

Albert laughed. 'It's work.'

Tamara's smile vanished faster than the sun behind an Ogmore rain cloud.

'Don't worry,' said Albert with a chuckle. 'It can wait. I'm happy here with you.'

Tamara's smile broke back through again.

'Would you like another cup of coffee?' she asked.

Albert finished off the last of his coffee and looked into the bottom of the cup.

'How many have we had so far?' he asked.

'Seven each. And one each at breakfast. And two with lunch.'

'Do you think that's too many?'

'I don't know,' said Albert. 'We're grown-ups. Grown-ups drink coffee.'

'We do, don't we?' said Tamara. She picked up Albert's empty cup along with her own and headed inside to buy more coffee.

Albert sat and watched the world go by. He had wanted to get a newspaper, but the lady in the post office had said that there weren't any today. No news, apparently. No news was good news. So, in the absence of a newspaper, Albert stretched out his legs and resolved to watch the world go by.

He watched the cars driving slowly along. He watched the birds circling over the sea. He watched the man dressed as a clown, riding on the back of another clown, stop outside the post office. He watched the man dressed as clown shove his fist through the post office window. He watched it explode, the glass flying in all directions. He watched the clown get back onto the other clown and disappear off down the street. He was shouting something about a girl, but Albert had stopped paying attention.

Tamara sat back down, placing a steaming mug of coffee down in front of Albert.

'Anything interesting happen while I was gone?' she asked,

'No,' said Albert. 'Nothing at all. All is well.'

Tamara smiled at Albert. Albert smiled at Tamara.

'What's all that glass?' asked Tamara.

'Oh, a clown came by, riding on the back of another clown, and smashed the post office window.'

Tamara took a slip of her coffee and winced as the hot liquid burned her lips.

Albert took a sip of his coffee. His was hot too. 'Do you think Lucy's OK?' he asked.

'What makes you ask that?' said Tamara.

'Just a feeling,' said Albert. 'Probably nothing.'

Lucy woke up in a strange bed in a room full of puppets. There were puppets on shelves on the wall, puppets hanging from the ceiling, puppets sitting in chairs. There were puppets everywhere.

'Lucy, you're awake!'

Hobo was sitting on the edge of the bed. He looked exhausted. 'Careworn' was what Lucy's mum would have called it. Punchinella was bustling about with an enamel bowl and towels. Lucy realised that there was a cold flannel on her forehead.

'What happened?' she asked.

'You fainted,' said Hobo. 'And you've got a

temperature.'

'Not sick,' said Punchinella, placing the bowl down on the floor by the side of the bed and sitting down next to Hobo. 'Is machine. Machine did this.'

Lucy tried to sit up. She felt weak and, just as before, like there was something missing. Something missing inside her, some crucial part. She felt hollowed out, like an old tree that had died and rotted inside, leaving only its bark.

'I feel strange,' she said. 'I feel like something's missing.'

Punchinella frowned. If everything that was happening had put a hundred years on Hobo, it was making the old Punch and Judy man younger by the second. He looked more alive than Lucy and Hobo put together.

'Lucy Wilson?' he asked. 'Who is she?'

Hobo gave Punchinella a puzzled look.

'You're looking at her.'

'No,' said Punchinella. 'Looking at Lucy Lethbridge-Stewart.'

'That's the same person,' insisted Hobo.

'Is it?' asked Punchinella. 'So you say. I not sure. Girl, what happened inside box?'

'You mean at the circus?' said Lucy. 'Well, I went inside the box and there were all these mirrors. Like a hall of mirrors, you know? Reflections everywhere. Then the reflections started to move on their own.

Like they were different to me, like they were other people. I remember my ring; it felt like it was on fire and…'

'Ring?' asked Punchinella.

Lucy lifted up her hand from under the covers and showed Punchinella her ring.

'It's sort of an heirloom, I guess,' she explained. 'Family gave it to me.'

'House,' said Hobo. 'It belongs to her house.'

Punchinella took Lucy's hand in his and brought the ring close to his face. He stared at it.

'Is not ring,' he said finally. 'Looks like ring, but is not ring. Is like Great Machine. From faraway place, faraway time. Is not ring, just hiding in shape of ring.'

Lucy snatched her hand away. 'It's my ring,' she said angrily. 'That's all.'

'So you say,' replied Punchinella. 'But I say ring saved you from machine. Machine cut Clown out from human, so machine could cut Wilson out from Lethbridge-Stewart. Only ring saved you, kept you here. Keeping you here now.'

'What does any of that mean?' said Lucy. She slumped back into the bed, frustration and fear overwhelming her. 'Just tell me something, anything that I can use… please.'

'I think I get it,' said Hobo quietly. 'I think I understand.'

Lucy turned her head to face Hobo. He still looked exhausted, but there was a spark of something in his eyes now. Lucy knew that spark. It was the lightning that ran through Hobo's brain.

'You tell everyone that you're Lucy Wilson, while to me you're Lucy Lethbridge-Stewart but… What if you're both? You're both Lucys. The machine was supposed to get rid of the bit of you that's Lethbridge-Stewart, and leave the rest behind.'

'But why?' asked Lucy. 'It doesn't make sense. Why not just, you know… do me in?'

'Because of who you are,' said Hobo. 'Think about it. Lucy Wilson goes to a mysterious circus and never comes back? People are going to ask questions. Your family are going to ask questions. But Lucy Wilson goes to a circus and comes back. Where's the crime? If your mum and dad even noticed that you'd stopped going on about aliens and monsters, they'd probably be happy about it. You'd be normal, just like everyone else. Earth is left without its defender, and nobody notices it happening.'

Lucy nodded. It made sense, even if she didn't want it to. As much as she believed she was Lucy Lethbridge-Stewart, as important as that side of her family was to her, there was no denying the rest of who she was too. The parts of her that came from her mum, even from her dad, who himself would have never have thought of himself as a Lethbridge-Stewart…. That was her too. She felt guilty that she'd made them less important to her than her grandfather and his legacy.

She now knew what was missing. It was the rest of her, the parts of Lucy Wilson that were just Lucy Wilson.

'When I met you,' said Punchinella, poking Hobo in the stomach, 'I said you were soft here. But soft here doesn't matter.'

He put his finger on Hobo's forehead. 'Strong here.'

He put his hand over Hobo's heart. 'Stronger here. Is why you see girl through clown. See girl when girl invisible. Is how you bring her back. Boy understands.'

Lucy gave the old man a sharp look. 'You could have explained this yourself, you know,' she said cooly. 'Maybe if you spoke proper English?'

'I speak languages you hear only in dreams,' replied Punchinella. 'Most of my words? No human has words for them.'

Lucy reached up for Hobo, wanting to pull herself upright again. Hobo's eyes opened wide as her hand drew close to him.

'Lucy!' he gasped. 'Your hand!'

Lucy stopped and stared at her hand. She could see through it, like it was made of dirty glass.

'Girl vanishing,' Punchinella said. 'Ring not keep her here forever.'

'There,' whispered Lucy, looking at her hand. 'But not there.'

Punchinella sniffed, sensing something in the air, and stood up suddenly from the bed.

'Take girl,' he snapped at Hobo. 'Boy understand now. Take girl and go.'

'Go?' said Hobo, 'Look at her! How can we go?'

Punchinella was already heading for the door. 'You must,' he replied. 'Harlequin is here.'

The mention of Harlequin's name electrified Lucy. She threw back the covers and hauled herself out of the bed. Unsteady, she grabbed a hold of Hobo.

'We're not ready,' she said, her voice weak. 'We don't know how to fight him.'

Hobo slipped an arm around Lucy, taking her weight. She felt so light, like she was barely there at all. They headed towards the door, Punchinella lumbering down the stairs ahead of them .

'We'll go to mine,' said Hobo. 'I'll call Mum.'

'No,' said Lucy, 'Hobo, you haven't seen them. There are clowns everywhere. Every house, every person. Everywhere.'

'You mean, my mum?'

'And mine. Every parent, every kid, every teacher.'

'So, where do we go?' asked Hobo. 'What do we

do?'

'I've got a plan,' said Lucy. 'It starts with hiding.'

'Right now,' said Hobo, 'hiding I can do.'

They reached the bottom of the stairs. Punchinella was waiting for them.

'Go through back door. No looking back.'

Hobo stalled. 'What about you?'

'I am Lord of this House. I am Punchinella. I cannot leave. Defend your own houses, I will defend mine. Now go!'

Hobo turned, taking Lucy with him, heading down the hallway. Behind them, something began pounding at the front door. They could hear laughter outside, someone calling out Punchinella's name. They pressed on through the kitchen, ignoring the crashing sounds behind them, ignoring the laughter.

'This isn't right,' said Hobo, turning the handle on the back door. It should have been dark outside, or raining, in some way ominous or foreboding. Ogmore greeted them with sunshine and a gentle sea breeze.

'I know,' said Lucy, 'but we'll make it right.'

Behind them, something metal clashed with something metal.

Lucy and Hobo left the House of Punchinella and disappeared into the warm sunshine of Ogmore.

— CHAPTER TWENTY-FIVE —

A CASTLE UNDER THE STARS

Hobo poked at the small fire he had made, encouraging the flames to dance a little higher. The fire wasn't giving up much warmth, but Hobo had a feeling that Lucy didn't need it. He could see the rough stone walls of Ogmore Castle through her; her body was becoming more translucent with each passing moment. The sun was going down and Hobo hoped that, somehow, his friend would look more solid in the moonlight.

Lucy had her back to Hobo, looking towards Ogmore. The two of them had barely made it out of town. Thankfully any clowns they had encountered had been directing their attentions at Punchinella's bungalow. Hobo could see them now. He supposed this was Punchinella's doing. His logical mind wasn't particularly geared towards the idea of invisible aliens that whispered in your ear, and he was even more unnerved by the idea of alien technology manipulating his senses.

'That's his place, isn't it?' said Lucy, pointing at a single plume of smoke rising up into the sunset. 'Punchinella's…'

'I guess so,' replied Hobo. 'Probably little more than ashes and timber now. Those clowns do a lot more than whisper.'

When he had suggested that they use Ogmore Castle as their secret rendezvous, it had seemed so much safer than it did now. It was a castle, after all. But looking around him at the crumbled old walls, all Hobo could think of was that any one of the hundred different shadows could be hiding a clown.

Hobo had accepted that life as Lucy's best friend would be dangerous, but apart from the Great Intelligence incident, so far it had been all secret bases and family secrets, walkie-talkies and codes. It had been a game. Now… it was game over.

His best friend was vanishing before his very eyes, and there was nothing he could do about it.

'Got any food in that bag?' asked Lucy, knocking Hobo's train of thought off its rails.

'Err, yeah, sure,' said Hobo. 'Of course.'

Hobo had hidden the bag in the castle months before, another piece of preparation, like the walkie-talkies and his super-secure computer. This one, however, was never supposed to be used. He'd even nicknamed it 'The Doomsday Bag'. He wished he hadn't now.

Stashed under a cairn of rocks, against a wall, the bag had remained hidden and undisturbed since the day Hobo had planted it. Now, its contents were the only tools and supplies that they had. Hobo groped around inside and pulled out a few shiny metal bags.

'Space meals,' he said proudly. 'As used by NASA and Mars Probe 20.'

He popped one of the bags open, a small cloud of dust shooting out.

'Instant chicken dinner. Just add water!'

'You've got water, right?' asked Lucy.

'Oh, yeah,' said Hobo. He rummaged around in the bag again and pulled out two sealed bottles of water. He opened both, placing one down in front of Lucy and one in front of himself. He tipped a packet of the space food to his lips and shuffled a mouthful of the dried food into his mouth.

It was not good.

Lucy covered her mouth, trying to hide her laughter as Hobo desperately guzzled water.

'It's good,' he mumbled, drying his chin on his sleeve. 'Just like the real thing.'

Lucy reached out for the water bottle.

'I'll take your word for it.'

But then she froze.

Hobo looked down at Lucy's hand. He could see the grass on the ground through it – not vaguely, like before, but crystal clear.

'Try,' he said gently, picking up the water bottle and offering it to Lucy. 'Try.'

Lucy reached for the water, her fingers trembling. Hobo held his breath as they closed around the water bottle. Not through it, not into it, but around it. Lucy held the bottle firmly. Smiling, she lifted it up to her lips.

'See, I told you that—'

The bottle hit the ground and rolled away from Lucy, still full of water.

'Sorry, Hobo.'

Hobo looked at his quickly vanishing friend. He had to do something.

'I've a phone,' he said suddenly. 'Curse me for an idiot!'

He delved into the rucksack, rummaging through the space meals and other paraphernalia he had packed in there. After a few moments, he pulled out an old fashioned mobile phone, a chunky looking thing with fat rubber buttons and a tiny screen.

'What is that?' asked Lucy incredulously. 'I thought you said you had a phone?'

'This is a phone,' replied Hobo. 'I wasn't going to pack a smartphone, not after what happened with the Great Intelligence. I got this old thing online. I guessed it wouldn't be powerful enough for the Intelligence to inhabit, but it still works. Battery lasts forever as well.'

Hobo turned on the phone, waiting patiently as it booted up and connected to the mobile network.

'See?' said Hobo, holding the small screen up to Lucy. 'Four bars!'

Hobo started keying in a number, the phone lighting up green as he pressed the rubber keys.

'You can't call my mum,' said Lucy urgently, 'or your parents. The clowns will hear.'

'I know,' replied Hobo. 'But I'm guessing the clowns haven't made it all the way to London yet. I reckon this is strictly an Ogmore problem. I memorised the number Dame Anne left us. If we call her, she can get a message to her husband and...'

'And Bob's your uncle!' said Lucy with a grin. She looked at the phone expectantly.

'Well?'

Hobo held the phone to his ear.

'It's ringing.'

They waited. A schoolboy and a ghost, huddled around a tiny fire in the ruins of Ogmore Castle. They waited as the phone rang... and rang, and rang, and rang. But there was no answer.

'Try again,' said Lucy.

Hobo hung up and dialled again, carefully entering the number digit by digit.

'You're sure you've got the right number?'

'100 percent,' said Hobo.

Lucy nodded. Even in a town taken over by clowns from outer space, there was no reason to doubt Hobo Kostinen's prodigious memory.

Hobo hung up and quickly dialled again.

'Come on, come on,' he muttered to himself.

Lucy listened intently, first to the ringing then, finally, to the sound of a voice at the other end of the line. She couldn't make out the words, but from the souring expression on Hobo's face, she guessed it wasn't what they wanted to hear.

Hobo threw the phone down on the grass, his teeth gritted in frustration.

'Just a message saying the number is not available.'

Hobo picked up the phone from where he'd dumped it, shoving it back into the rucksack along with the water and the space-meals.

'So that's it,' he said sullenly. 'No help. We're on our own.'

Lucy got up and walked back to the wall of the castle. The sky had turned a deep, fleshy purple now, like a bruise. Ogmore was a faint glow of street lights and a single wisp of smoke on the horizon.

'No,' said Lucy. Her voice was firm. Hobo recognised the tone. It was the tone she used when her mind was made up and any hope you had of changing it was somewhere several miles out at sea. 'We're not on our own. There's one person who might be able to help us.'

'Who?' asked Hobo.

Lucy turned, her face set. 'Isn't it obvious, Hobo? Me!'

— CHAPTER TWENTY-SIX —

THE OTHER LUCY

Lucy Wilson sat in her bedroom and read over the most recent entry in her diary. It had certainly been a difficult day and a lot of things were refusing to make sense.

Dear Diary,

Another lovely day in Ogmore!

The weather was lovely today and Dad made me a lovely breakfast. It is lovely having Dad home from London (which is a horrible place that smells and that I never want to go back to ever). We are hoping to do something lovely together on the weekend, like maybe go to the circus (which I have never been to before, ever, no matter what anyone says).

~~Breakfast was disrupted slightly by someone breaking into my room.~~

Nothing peculiar happened at breakfast.

I had a lovely walk to the school bus this morning. I met all of my lovely friends there, but I also ran into Hobo (who is not to be trusted and who I should stay away from). Hobo was very distracted on the bus, playing with his walkie-talkie, and totally not noticing that I had changed my hair and make-up. Boys!

Anyway, today was extra special because there was a school trip to see the most amazing and lovely show, Punch and Judy! This is the greatest story of all, and all school children should know it (and soon will).

~~*The show was disrupted when a girl who looked like me in clown make-up appeared, caused a ruckus, and disappeared with the lost Prince of House Punchinella.*~~

Nothing happened to disrupt the show at all and it was lovely.

I returned to school for some lovely lessons in the afternoon. We learnt about history, although nothing especially interesting or important appears to have happened at any point in the past. Everyone got an A+ on their essays from last week, which was lovely.

I came home on the bus. Hobo wasn't there but three other boys smiled at me. Boys!

~~*Search parties are looking for Hobo everywhere, the streets are not safe.*~~

~~*Who was that girl at the Punch and Judy show? She looked just like me.*~~

~~*Why do I keep writing things down and then crossing them out?*~~

I'm planning a lovely evening now of writing in my diary and other related activities.

Lucy frowned at the diary entry. Something about it didn't seem right. Actually, nothing about it seemed right at all. It was as if it had been written by someone else, someone with only a very vague idea of what secrets girls commit to their diaries, especially girls like Lucy Wilson. She flicked back a page to the previous entry. That one didn't have any corrections, seemed far less concerned with hair and make-up, and had a shortlist of teachers most likely to be vulnerable to outer-space-parasite mind control. Lucy Wilson didn't know why, but that diary entry felt far more like 'her' than the previous one.

A noise outside startled her and, without knowing why, she quickly closed her diary and put it back in its hiding place, behind some other books on her bookshelf, safely out of sight. Her room had been cleaned during the day, presumably by Mum.

Something pinged against the glass of Lucy's bedroom window. She stood up immediately and was halfway across the room to take a look outside when she found herself saying, 'I should ignore that and go to bed.'

She frowned. Thoughts like that had been popping into her head all day. Thoughts she didn't really recognise but that seemed to be somehow more powerful than her normal thoughts. It was like trying to hold a conversation in the middle of a concert; she literally could not hear herself think.

She took another step towards the window. Another. There was a second ping against the glass.

'There's nobody there,' Lucy Wilson said. 'I don't need to go to the window. I should go to bed.'

But then something inside her flared: the old Lucy Wilson temper. She forced herself across the room and, with trembling hands, she reached for the curtains.

'I'm going to regret this,' she said to herself.

And she was right.

'Lucy, we can't stand around all night tossing stones at your window,' hissed Hobo, crouching down behind the Wilson house garden hedge. 'What if she's not in?'

'I'm in,' said Lucy. 'I can feel it. Now, throw another.'

Hobo reluctantly picked up another pebble from under the hedge and pitched it up at the window. It struck the glass with a resounding ping.

'Look, both your mum and dad are in there. What if they come out?'

Lucy raised a ghostly eyebrow at Hobo.

'How many times have we done this, Hobo?' she asked. 'They never come out.'

'Never is a poor man's word for not-so-far,' Hobo replied. 'Just because it hasn't happened yet, doesn't mean it can't ever happen.'

'Good point,' said Lucy. 'I'll take it into consideration. In the meantime, fire again, Mr Kostinen!'

Hobo sighed and did as he was told. He'd seen Lucy scale the porch and clamber in through her bedroom window as easily as other people sat down on a park bench, but in her current state neither of them trusted her abilities. For all Hobo knew, Lucy could disappear completely or fall through to the centre of the Earth at any moment. But for her part, at least, Lucy was staying upbeat. Remarkably upbeat in fact. Hobo would have ribbed about her 'Lethbridge-Stewart' showing, but it wasn't the time. But then again, it might never be the time again.

'I see something,' whispered Lucy, pointing up at the window.

Hobo looked up and saw it too. A shadow behind the curtains.

'One last time, Hobo,' said Lucy eagerly. 'We've got my attention.'

Hobo picked another pebble up from the ground, but he didn't get a chance to throw it. A floor above, Not-Lucy threw open the curtains and looked down at them. Behind her was a clown.

'Oh no,' breathed Hobo. 'He's seen us.'

'Yep,' said Lucy, smiling. 'Now we've got him.'

'Got him?' said Hobo with a gasp. 'When were

we planning to "get him"? Is that your plan?'

Lucy grinned at Hobo. 'I don't have a plan, Hobo. I'm Lucy Lethbridge-Stewart, remember? Alien busting is in my blood. It's instinct.'

'And?'

'And I'm thinking she's got a little of that instinct too.'

Lucy looked up at her alter-ego, the Lucy who wore make-up and did her hair, the Lucy who fitted in. The Lucy who Lucy would be with all the other bits taken out. When Lucy, the original Lucy, had first seen her, she'd called her a dummy. Now she looked like something more than that. She reminded Lucy of Pinocchio – the puppet who came to life, but who longed to be real.

'She sees you,' whispered Hobo.

He was right. Not-Lucy was looking back, and somehow, somewhere between the two girls, there was a connection. Lucy could feel it in the air. They were like magnets pulling towards each other.

'Behind you!' shouted Lucy, so suddenly that it made Hobo jump.

Lucy's alter-ego jumped as well, snapping out of her reverie. She spun around and, for the first time, she saw a clown.

Hobo winced, expecting the quiet of the night to be shattered by a scream.

It wasn't.

Hobo opened his eyes just in time to see the other Lucy Wilson punching the clown square on the nose.

'That's my girl,' said Lucy.

'Yeah,' agreed Hobo. 'That's you all right.'

— CHAPTER TWENTY-SEVEN —

HARLEQUIN
TRIUMPHANT

It was already night by the time Harlequin returned to the circus.

The crowds would be arriving soon, eager for another performance. Harlequin felt ready to give one. There was nothing like a kill to clear away the cobwebs. It make him feel like a new clown. Killing Punchinella had not been easy; the old man had put up a fight. But it had to be done. The House of Punchinella was finally, and forever, no more.

Art was waiting under the lights at circus entrance.

'I have returned victorious, my darlings!' crowed Harlequin, hopping down from the back of the clown he had been riding. He patted the creature's flank and watched admiringly as it padded away on all fours.

'The girl, my lord?' asked Art.

Harlequin's face soured. From his belt, he pulled

out a crumpled and torn mask. He threw it at Art's feet.

'Far greater prey,' he said with a sneer. 'The last Prince of the House of Punchinella.'

Art picked up the mask and turned it over in his hands, examining it carefully.

'He is dead.'

'Dead and buried,' replied Harlequin. 'We brought his house down.'

He began to laugh at his own joke, but a slow hand-clap cut him short. With a snarl on his face he spun around to see who dared interrupt him in his moment of triumph.

A clown dressed all in white, except for the black trim and black buttons of his jacket, stepped from the shadows. He wore a tall, pointed hat, also adorned with large black buttons. His face, pale and ghostly, picked up the colours of the circus lights. He smiled, but it was a sad smile, matching the single black tear drop tattooed on his cheek.

'Bravo!' said the clown. His voice was high, and slow, and sad. It sounded like the voice of somebody singing at a funeral.

'Pierrot,' growled Harlequin.

'Harlequin,' crooned Pierrot. 'How wonderful to see you again. When did I last have the pleasure? Not since, oh, let me think…'

'When we burned down the Chapels of the Eight

Sisters,' said Harlequin. It was a story that normally Harlequin loved to tell, but at this moment it barely brought a smile to his face. His eyes were on Art, and if they had been billboards they would have been advertising a two-for-one special on murder.

Pierrot put this arm around Harlequin. 'Oh yes, of course. That was a lovely afternoon.' The white-clad clown guided him away from Art, leading him into the circus. 'Now,' he said, his voice suddenly serious. 'You must tell me everything that has been going on.'

Art watched as the two clowns, both high princes of their houses, disappeared arm in arm into the tents. There was a very real chance that he would never see Harlequin again. Killers, no matter how flamboyant, had their limits. Pierrot was something altogether more dangerous indeed.

Pierrot was a politician.

'Off you go,' said Lucy.

'What?'

'Off you go,' she repeated. 'Go and get her.'

Hobo had a feeling Lucy would have given him a push if it weren't for the fact her hand might have passed right through him. He gave her a sideways look.

'Why me?'

Lucy raised a ghostly eyebrow.

'Hi, Dad, just me, the ghostly doppelganger of your daughter who you thought was upstairs.'

'Fair enough,' said Hobo. 'I'll go and get her.'

He walked up to the front door, waited for Lucy to duck out of sight behind the side of the porch, and rang the bell.

A light went on somewhere inside and a shadowy figure approached the door.

Hobo wasn't sure what would be more frightening – a clown, or Lucy's mother at this time of night.

The front door swung open.

'Hello, Mr Wilson,' said Hobo, stretching an awkward smile across his face.

Albert Wilson eyed Hobo suspiciously. Hobo had always suspected that Lucy's father disliked the fact that Hobo had been involved in the whole Great Intelligence affair. He had the feeling Albert blamed him for encouraging the Lethbridge-Stewart side of his daughter.

'Hobo,' said Albert. He was speaking slowly, like Hobo was some long forgotten relative that he had bumped into at a wedding. Hobo realised that Mr Wilson was dressed up, as if he was going somewhere: a smart suit, a snazzy shirt with an open collar; he even had some fancy socks on his feet.

'Hello, Mr Wilson,' said Hobo, repeating himself slowly. 'Is Lucy in?'

Albert clicked his fingers, seeming suddenly to remember something.

'Hobo!' he said. 'We've got our eyes out for you!' He grabbed the boy by the shoulders and hauled him bodily in through the door. It slammed shut, leaving Lucy trapped outside.

Lucy ran up to the door and peeped in through one of the glass panels. Her dad was leading Hobo forcefully down the hall. She wondered if she had faded away enough to pass right through the door.

'I'm here, but not here,' she muttered to herself, hoping for a moment of Lethbridge-Stewart inspiration.

'Lucy...'

Lucy took a few steps backwards, looking up at the house.

'Lucy...'

Lucy Wilson, her head poking from an open window, smiled. Lucy Lethbridge-Stewart smiled back.

'I'm here *and* there,' said Lucy Lethbridge-Stewart.

'What do I do?' hissed Not-Lucy.

'Where's the clown?'

'In the mirror.'

'Go downstairs,' Lucy Lethbridge-Stewart pleaded in a whisper. 'Help Hobo.'

'Help Hobo,' the doppelganger repeated. A second later, she was gone.

Hobo was being manhandled down the hallway and into the lounge. Mrs Wilson was there, dressed to the nines just like Mr Wilson perched on the edge of the sofa. The coffee table was living up to its name; there were more empty mugs and coffee cups on there than Hobo cared to count. Mr Wilson looked absolutely wired. Hobo thought that he could almost see her vibrating, as if she were being pumped with electricity.

'Hobo!' shouted Mrs Wilson 'Great to see you. We've been keeping an eye out for you. We have to. That's important. Very important. We're not to let you out of our sight. That's important. We're going to the circus tonight. Do you like the circus? We think it's marvellous, don't we, Albert? Ignore him, he thinks it's marvellous, of course he does, everyone does, don't they? Well, anyway, we're going tonight because tonight is special. Have you seen the flyers? Of course you have, everyone has, everyone knows. Tonight is the night, Hobo. Tonight is the night. You must come with us! Then we can keep an eye on you and not let you out of our sight.

Mrs Wilson was talking so fast that Hobo could barely keep up with what she was saying. Back with Mrs Wilson, Mr Wilson seemed to have picked up speed as well, nodding and saying, 'Yes, yes, yes,' at every microscopic pause in her rapid-fire speech.

'You're going to the circus?' Hobo said slowly, hoping to take the pace of the conversation down a notch. 'And is Lucy going with you?'

'Of course I am, Hobo.'

Hobo turned. Behind him, standing in the doorway was Not-Lucy. She was dressed up for a night out as well, her face made-up and her hair styled.

She winked an exaggerated wink at him.

Wilsons all around him, Hobo felt surrounded. 'I should really speak to my parents,' he said nervously. 'They will want to know where I am.'

'You'll be at the circus,' replied Mr Wilson and Mr Wilson in perfect unison.

'You'll be at the circus,' said Not-Lucy.

'Everyone's going.'

'Everyone's going.'

Lucy slipped her hand into Hobo's and gave it a squeeze.

'Everyone's going,' she said. '*Everyone.*'

Hobo took a deep breath and hoped, hoped, hoped that she meant what he thought she meant.

'Everyone's going,' he replied, feigning excitement.

'Great!' said Mr Wilson, clapping his hands together. 'We can keep an eye on you.'

'I'll keep an eye on him,' said Not-Lucy, yanking Hobo towards the doorway.

'Where are you two off to now?' asked Mrs Wilson.

'I need Hobo's help with something,' said Not-Lucy.

Hobo winced. It was the kind of vague answer that to any parent was like a juicy lamb chop dangled in front of a predator. His Lucy, the normal Lucy, was far better at coming up with excuses.

Mr and Mrs Wilson looked at each other blankly. It seemed like they were both waiting for the other one to say something. After a few a painful seconds, they said in unison…

'OK.'

Not-Lucy didn't waste a second, dragging Hobo down the hallway and straight up the stairs.

'What are you doing?' hissed Hobo.

'I need your help,' replied Not-Lucy. 'Help. Hobo. Help.'

Hobo shook his head. For a moment Lucy's doppelganger had almost seemed normal, but now she was acting all Not-Lucy again. Maybe she was breaking down in the same way that his Lucy was fading away. There wasn't time to ponder this; a second later he was being dragged into Lucy's bedroom.

Hobo didn't know what he had been expecting,

but Lucy's bedroom was a surprise. It barely looked lived in at all: there were still some cardboard boxes that hadn't been unpacked, and clothes hung on the back of the door in transparent plastic wrapping. It felt… temporary, like Lucy didn't believe she would be there long. Hobo swallowed down a sick feeling in his stomach as he realised that, if they didn't find a way to stop Lucy from fading away, she might be right.

Lucy Wilson wouldn't be there anymore.

'Mirror,' said Not-Lucy, spinning Hobo around.

Hobo stood facing Lucy's dressing table and looked into the mirror.

A clown, the clown that Not-Lucy had punched, looked back from behind the glass.

Hobo yelped, jumping back startled, patting himself down. But the clown in the mirror didn't copy his movements, didn't seem connected to him at all. It just stood, and stared, and pressed its hands against the glass.

'Like Alice,' muttered Hobo. 'Through the looking glass. It's trapped on the other side of the mirror.'

'He fell through,' said Not-Lucy. 'When I hit him.'

Hobo approached the mirror slowly. The clown was scratching at the glass now. Hobo was sure he could hear the sound of its nails scraping against the transparent barrier, just on the very edge of his hearing. Whatever it was that separated here from there, he hoped it was thick enough.

The clown suddenly took a few steps back and then charged at the glass. The mirror rattled, the dressing table shifted a few inches forwards, but the clown was knocked backwards.

'I don't think he can get out,' said Hobo. 'He's like a mime trapped in an invisible box.'

What was it Punchinella had said, in his story, about the first clowns?

'Clown was born when man first looked at himself,' said Hobo, turning the facts over in his mind.

Was this the way to defeat them? Could it really be that simple?

'What do we do?' asked Not-Lucy.

Hobo chewed the end of his thumb for a second, his mind whirring.

'The only thing we can do,' he replied. 'We go to the circus.'

Not-Lucy turned and headed towards the door.

'But we're going to take a little detour,' added Hobo. 'There's something we need.'

CHAPTER TWENTY-EIGHT

THE FORBIDDEN WORLD OF GIRLS' CHANGING ROOMS

Pierrot and Harlequin faced each other from opposite ends of a long, polished table. Pierrot never travelled anywhere alone. His seemingly infinite entourage of servants, helpers, and general hangers-on delivered an endless assortment of food to the table.

There were bird-like creatures the size of roast chickens, but with ten legs, that came on a bed of orange and black vegetables. There were jellies that moved, not just with a wobble, but with fat little jelly legs up and down the table, depositing piles of sugared fruits every few steps. There was a fish that ran half the length of the table and then curved back on itself, so that its gawping mouth swallowed up its meaty tail. And all around there were bowls of every possible size and shape, all filled to the brim with treats and delicacies from around the galaxy: sour nuts from the spice mines of Pedula 4; from Karakis Majora, musical fruit that sang as you ate them; marsh minnows, a kind of newt eaten live, from Thoros Beta; sweet apples from Epsilon Eriadani B, delicious after dark but poisonous if eaten during the daytime; gumblejack, one of the tastiest fish from all of Mutter's Spiral; and worms from the not-quite-lost moon of Bajura, which would crawl into a person's mouth of their own accord, if said person should sit still long enough.

In pride of place, raised up above all the others, was the greatest of all clown delicacies: jelly babies.

Almost everything at the feast displeased Pierrot, except the jelly babies.

'You've caused quite a stir at home, you know?' he said lazily.

'Have I?' replied Harlequin. 'Do tell.'

'This little adventure of yours. The houses are not best pleased.'

Harlequin sneered. 'The houses will do nothing.'

'I would not be so sure,' said Pierrot. 'We have tolerated your antics thus far because, despite yourself, you have been useful to us. This little troupe of yours, it's handy to have around sometimes. It's the perfect place to send our undesirables, the idiots and the clods and the extra children that clutter up the place.'

'Yet none from your own house?'

'My house has no undesirables. Any Pierrott in your troupe are there... at my bidding,' replied Pierrot, coldly.

'Perhaps,' said Harlequin, 'or perhaps you are all just equally undesirable. You just can't see the dead wood for the trees.'

Pierrot picked up a piece of fruit from the table, something similar to a banana but bright blue and twice the size. He pressed a long finger nail into the flesh and slowly peeled away the skin. The juice that dripped out was a deep crimson. Pierrot licked it from the tip of his finger.

'Past its best,' he said, tossing the strange fruit down the table to Harlequin. Harlequin batted it away, chuckling as one of Pierrot's many retainers scuttled out of the shadows to retrieve it from the dusty floor.

'Others may be happy with crumbs from your table, but I have loftier aspirations.'

'You're a murderer, Harlequin. Worse than that, you're a paid murderer. You do not kill for sport or for art, you kill for coin. Clown does not work. Clown does not slave. Clown is simply... clown.'

'Clown is mostly idiots,' said Harlequin. He hopped up from his chair and sprang gracefully onto the table. 'I have travelled from one end of this universe to the other,' he said, stalking towards

Pierrot, placing his feet daintily amongst the constantly changing array of food. 'And I have seen so many, many things. It was Harlequin who found the Many Edged Blade. It was Harlequin who cut, and stitched, and gouged, and sculpted himself into something unique among clown. It was Harlequin who formed the Great Troupe, and made name of clown feared by children on a thousand, thousand worlds.'

Harlequin stopped, his feet either side of Pierrot's plate. There was no applause. Around him, Pierrot's retainers and servants continued to bustle. Harlequin's lip twisted into a sneer.

'I said—'

'Not all children,' interrupted Pierrot.

'What?'

'I said… not all children.'

Harlequin looked down at Pierrot, his face twitching with rage.

'The girl, Lucy they call her. She escaped you. She *bested* you. You thought you had her, but she got away. Because not all children are scared of you, of clown. And neither am I.'

Harlequin's hand twitched. He could feel the weight of his blade in its sheaf. How easy it would have been to cut Pierrot off mid-sentence. But that would really spoil the fun.

'Oh, Pierrot, you really are too much!' Harlequin

bent his knees, then sprang into the air, somersaulting over Pierrot's head and landing without a sound behind him. His mouth was at Pierrot's ear before the other clown could even react. 'This game is bigger than you can imagine, Pierrot. I killed the last Prince of Punchinella. I will kill the girl when next I see her. I may just kill you to make it a nice round three. Not for coin, of course. Just for sport.'

'There would be war,' said Pierrot with a gulp.

'The Clown Wars?' mused Harlequin. 'You know, I think that has a certain… pizzazz.'

Hobo sat in the back of Mr Wilson's car, making the most awkward small talk of his life.

Not-Lucy was next to him, grinning away inanely. Hobo couldn't tell if she was as barmy as her parents appeared to be, or if she was playing pretend for cover. Either way there was something deeply *weird* about her.

He almost envied the real Lucy, who, assuming she hadn't faded away to nothing already, was hiding in the boot.

It had been a simple ruse: he'd asked to put his rucksack into the boot of the car, and Not-Lucy had kept Mr Wilson busy as Lucy crept across from behind the bushes and clambered in. She'd only had time to mouth, 'What's happening,' at him, and he had only been able to give her a reassuring smile. The truth was he didn't know the answer, not completely. But he did have the beginnings of a plan.

Mr Wilson brought the car to a halt outside the school gates.

'See,' said Mrs Wilson 'It's all locked up.'

'We've got a way in, haven't we, Lucy?' said Hobo.

'Yes,' replied the doppelganger. 'We've got a way in.'

'Hmm,' grumbled Mrs Wilson. 'I'm not sure how I feel about you having a secret entrance to your school.'

'Well,' began Hobo, 'we really only use it in emergencies and—'

'No,' interrupted Mrs Wilson. 'I mean I literally don't know how I feel about it. I should probably have an opinion. Albert?'

Mr Wilson looked across at his wife blankly. 'I was hoping you'd have one.'

'Do we need coffee?'

Hobo sighed and let himself out of the car. 'We'll be right back.'

'We'll be right back,' confirmed Not-Lucy, clambering across the back seat and following Hobo out of the door.

Hobo popped open the boot. Lucy, the real Lucy looked up at them both.

'I am not overly happy,' she whispered, 'that I'm

in the boot with a rucksack, spare tyre, and whatever Dad forgot to file last time he was at the office.'

'Needs must,' said Hobo, helping her out. She felt as light as a feather.

'Hello, Lucy.'

Not-Lucy looked at Lucy. Lucy looked back at Not-Lucy.

'This is awkward,' said Hobo. 'Awkward and weird. Awk-weird.'

'Why are we here?' asked Lucy.

'We need to steal something,' replied Hobo. 'Follow me.'

Leaving the boot open to block Lucy's parents view, he scurried off along the chain link fence to the spot he and Lucy had escaped through after school just a few days ago.

Lucy paused for a moment. If whatever was happening to her couldn't be reversed, if this long and slow fading away was how she was to leave the world, she wondered if this might be her last chance to speak to her parents. There were a lot of things she would like to say to them, if she was about to disappear. A lot of things she'd like to apologise for too.

'Follow me!' said Not-Lucy suddenly, breaking her train of thought.

Lucy gritted her teeth. 'Follow my foot up your... ah, what's the point.'

Hobo, Lucy, and Not-Lucy vanished down the side of the fence, through the gap, and into school.

'All right, Captain Confusing,' said Lucy, as Hobo prised open the door to the swimming pool. 'What is it that we need so desperately that we've come to school to steal it?'

'Mirrors,' said Hobo, as he disappeared inside. 'Mirrors.'

Not-Lucy opened her mouth but, before she could speak, Lucy put her almost translucent hand over it.

'Don't,' she said sharply. 'Don't repeat everything he says.'

Not-Lucy nodded and Lucy took her hand away.

'Don't repeat everything he says.'

Lucy grumbled to herself, pushing past Not-Lucy with what little mass she had left to muster. She followed Hobo into the darkness of the swimming pool.

She found him at the door to the girls' changing rooms, awkwardly shuffling from one foot to another.

'What's wrong?' she called.

'It just… feels a bit weird,' said Hobo. 'I'm not supposed to go into the girls' changing room.'

'Oh for pity's sake! We're supposed to be saving the world. I'm sure it's allowed for world-saving purposes!'

'Can you go into the boys?'

Lucy looked at the door to the boys changing room, then back to Hobo.

'No,' she said reluctantly. 'But that's different.'

'Why?'

'Boys smell,' she said. 'Well-known fact. Everyone knows it.'

'Everyone knows it.'

Not-Lucy's shoulders sank. 'Is she going to be with us the whole time?'

'She's part of you, Lucy. You said so yourself.'

'She's a very annoying part.'

'Case closed then.'

Not-Lucy punched Hobo in the arm.

'Oi!'

'Thanks,' said Lucy, smiling at her double. 'We can't keep calling her "her" or "it" though. We have to give her a name.'

Hobo scrunched up his face. 'What if I call you Number One and her Number Two?'

'No!' said both girls in unison.

'All right, how about…'

'Lucy Wilson,' said Not-Lucy, interrupting Hobo's chain of thought.

'No, I'm Lucy Wilson,' said the original Lucy.

'No you're not,' said the copy. 'That's not what you call yourself.'

Lucy looked at her copy. This time, she really looked at her. The better hair, the better dress sense, the light touch of make-up. This was the Lucy she always thought people wanted her to be, but which she could never quite manage.

'Wilson,' said Hobo. 'That's what we should call her.'

'And what will you call me?' asked Lucy.

'Lucy,' replied Hobo. 'Lethbridge-Stewart sounds grand all right, but it's a bit of a mouthful. I'll call you Lucy and her Wilson. I like it, it's... snappy.'

'Like Hobo?'

Hobo smiled. 'Exactly!'

Wilson wandered to the edge of the pool, looking down into the water. Lucy and Hobo watched her. There was a touch of electricity in the air, the friction of the moment conjuring static out of nothingness. Lucy wasn't sure if she was looking at the birth of a new person or the birth of another monster.

'It feels like...' she whispered to Hobo.

'I know,' he whispered back. 'Frankenstein.'

'I was going to say "we should get started".'

'Oh.'

Quietly, slowly, Lucy and Hobo opened the door to the girls' changing rooms.

— CHAPTER TWENTY-NINE —
COSTUMES

The journey to the circus was a lot less awkward. The newly anointed Wilson seemed to have discovered a previously undiscovered enthusiasm for conversation – particularly about nothing at all. The weather. What was happening outside the car window. Hobo's choice of socks. Nothing passed without Wilson's comment. Her long, *detailed* comment. In the rare moments when she did stop talking, Hobo was convinced he could hear sniggering coming from the boot.

Finally, Mr Wilson brought the car to a halt, bumping it up on a grass verge a short walk from the circus. All the normal parking spaces were filled, and other cars were already joining them up on the verge.

'Looks like the whole town is here,' said Mr Wilson.

'The whole town *is* here,' said Mrs Wilson. 'Everyone's going.'

'Everyone's going,' said Hobo, right on cue.

Wilson gave him a sideways look.

They clambered out of the car.

'I'll lock the car up, Mr Wilson,' Hobo offered, reaching out a hand for the keys. 'You'll want to get on ahead and get a good seat, right?'

Albert Wilson narrowed his eyes. 'I'm supposed to keep an eye on you,' he said.

'I'll keep an eye on him,' said Wilson, linking her arm with Hobo's. 'Besides, the entire town is here. We're *all* supposed to keep an eye on him.'

Mr Wilson shrugged. 'OK. Be careful walking up in the dark though.'

He tossed Hobo the keys and, linking his own arm with Mrs Wilson's, headed off to towards the circus. Hobo and Wilson waited a moment for the coast to clear, then popped open the boot.

Lucy was waiting inside. She looked more solid in the darkness, but as she climbed out of the car, Hobo could see that she was not steady on her feet. Wilson put an arm around her, holding her up while Hobo pulled his bulging rucksack out of the boot.

'Are you sure you're up to this?' he asked Lucy, swinging the pack onto his back.

'The show must go on, Hobo,' she said. 'I'll be fine once I've had some air.'

Hobo knew he couldn't have changed her mind even if he'd really wanted to. 'Come on then,' he said. 'Let's find somewhere to get changed.'

Somewhere to get changed ended up being behind a large unkempt hedgerow not far from the entrance to the circus. There were clowns everywhere, but they were all occupied guiding their respective humans into the circus. Lucy and Wilson kept a careful eye on them as Hobo explained his plan.

'In your bedroom,' he began. 'Wilson has trapped a clown in the mirror.'

'Go on,' said Lucy.

'In Pete's… In Punchinella's story, the many-faced clown, whoever he is, he got the clowns to leave Earth by showing them their selves.'

'So you think the clowns are afraid of mirrors?'

'No, I think mirrors are where they are from. The story said clowns were created when man looked at himself. I think they're from the other side of the mirror.'

'Like *Alice in Wonderland*?'

'Well, *Through the Looking Glass* would be more accurate, but yes.'

'Doesn't make sense,' said Lucy. 'We'd see them all the time.'

'Would we?' asked Hobo. 'We don't see other aliens all the time, but you keep telling me they're everywhere. I saw this with my own eyes, Lucy. And think about Punchinella's house too.'

'What about it?'

'There were mirrors everywhere. I thought maybe he was just really, *really* vain or something, but what if they were for defence? Self defence.'

'Like a barricade.'

Hobo unzipped his rucksack and lifted out one of the mirrors that the trio had stolen from the girls' changing rooms.

'More like armour,' he said. 'Watch.'

And, with that, he got to work. He pulled a spool of strong blue twine out of the rucksack and began to make loops with it. The mirrors had been screwed to the changing room walls. Hobo's electric screwdriver, another of the rucksack's offerings, had made short work of the screws, leaving each mirror with a conveniently placed hole in each corner.

It didn't take Hobo long to fashion two suits of what he very loosely called armour – a pair of mirrors that could be worn on the front and back, like a sandwich board man's sign, held in place by the blue twine. He hefted the first one onto himself, and offered the other to Lucy.

'It's not too heavy,' said Hobo. 'I'll just help you lift it on.'

'Wait!' said Lucy. 'What if I'm still like them? What if I go into the mirror as well?'

'That won't happen,' said Hobo confidently. 'Punchinella got the clown off you. Or out of you. However it works.'

'You're the one who says we should always think things through, Hobo. We need to be sure about this!'

Hobo could have kicked himself. Lucy was right. He'd let his actions get ahead of his brain, exactly what he was always criticising her for. The suit of armour might just prove the death of the person he was trying to save.

'Err,' he hesitated, 'maybe we could...'

'I'll do it,' interrupted Wilson.

'What?' Hobo and Lucy replied in unison.

'We're parts of the same whole,' said Wilson, matter-of-factly. 'If it's safe for me, it will be safe for you.'

'I'm not sure that make sense,' said Hobo.

'I think it does,' said Lucy quietly.

Hobo looked at the two girls. They faced him with identical expressions – an expression that he had learned meant that the conversation was over.

'Lethbridge-Stuart intuition?' he suggested.

'Wilson intuition,' corrected Wilson. 'Never fails.'

Lucy shrugged. Hobo shrugged back and lifted the second set of armour up and over Wilson. For a moment, nothing happened. Then, slowly but surely, nothing continued to happen.

As one Hobo, Lucy and Wilson let out a single sigh of relief.

'Told you,' said Wilson.

'Totally fine,' said Lucy.

'Nothing to worry about,' said Wilson.

Hobo shook his head at Wilson. 'I think I liked you better when you repeated everything I said.'

'Hey!' said Lucy, throwing an arm around Wilson. 'Leave other me alone!'

'Two of you,' muttered Hobo, stringing together a third set of armour. 'Is the world ready?'

'Let's hope not,' said Wilson. 'Now, let's get in there and find us some clowns!'

CHAPTER THIRTY

INSTRUCTIONS ON
HOW TO STEAL
A WORLD

Pierrot stood in his tent and watched as the humans filed into the Big Top, their clown counterparts at their sides. Pantalones and Dotores mostly, they whispered and nudged and guided their human charges like gentle, devoted parents.

Art stood beside Pierrot, awaiting his command.

'Humans,' mused Pierrot. 'I wonder what it was we were supposed to be so afraid of?'

'The troupe are bonded to them,' said Art. 'They cannot leave.'

'Small price for a world,' said Pierrot. 'Can you imagine a more gentle invasion?'

'I suppose not,' replied Art. 'But this is just one small town. You cannot mean to take the whole world this way?'

Pierrot turned to face Art, his eyes cold. Art had

grown used to Harlequin's moods, in particular his rages and his furies, but Pierrot was a very different kind of fish. A cold fish, and a cowardly fish, and a poisonous one as well. Harlequin came at you with his hands, or his knife, and he let you know he was coming with an elaborate flourish. But Art suspected that by the time you realised Pierrot intended to do away with you, you were already quite dead.

'One small town today. Another next year. Another after that. Inch by inch, person by person. We take this world so slowly that the humans don't realise it is happening. The art of invasion, Art, is to be boring. The art of invasion is to be normal, the new normal. Eventually the people you control outnumber the people that you don't, and then the people you don't control are the strange ones, the outcasts… the clowns. The world will cast them out to defend itself, and give itself over to you willingly.'

Art gave an involuntary shudder.

'There's nothing to be afraid of,' continued Pierrot. 'It's almost… natural. Consider it evolution. Human and clown were once one. They will be again.'

'But with clown in control?'

'Of course,' said Pierrot. 'We are the more sophisticated. What other choice could there be?'

Art saw something that might just have been a smile pass across Pierrot's face.

'My lord, when I sent my message, begging your help, it was to save the other members of my troupe. Your plan condemns them; it leaves them trapped here forever.'

'Your point being?' asked Pierrot.

'My lord, they are clown,' implored Art.

Whatever small smile Pierrot might have worn vanished. He ran his tongue under his lips as if he was trying to get rid of the taste of something sour.

'Are they?' he asked, his voice low and edged with malice. 'They are outcasts of their houses, followers of one who turned his back on us. They are the inconvenient, the broken, the unwanted. When I look at them I do not see clown. I see slave.'

Art took a step back from Pierrot.

The sad-faced clown took a step forwards, pressing Art back into the shadows.

'And when you look at me, my lord?'

'When I look at you?' sneered Pierrot. 'Oh, Art, when I look at you I see something that is less clown than any of them. What are you, eh? A patchwork man? An experiment? A pet for Harlequin? I'll tell you what I see when I look at you. I see something strange, I see something unusual. I see something that will stand out. Something that will get their attention.'

'I... am clown, Lord Pierrot. I was... I am... Dotore. I remain loyal to my house and to yours.'

'You are not clown,' said Pierrot. 'You are meat that Harlequin scraped off the blade of his knife. You just happened to end up in the in the shape of clown. You are nothing. You are not here.'

Art felt a strange sensation move through his body, as if every part of him had in a flash moved an extra millimetre apart. His vision blurred, darkness pushing in from the sides, leaving only Pierrot's stark white face and dark eyes before him.

'I… am…' gasped Art. He had never taken the time to ask Harlequin if he had lungs or not, after he had been remade. 'I… am…'

'You are not here,' hissed Pierrot.

Art fell to the floor. He watched as his legs unravelled, as he literally came apart at the seams, leaving only rags on the muddy ground.

'*I… am…*'

'You are not here,' hissed Pierrot again. 'You are not in this story anymore.'

Art tried to grab a hold of the prince, but his fingers were nothing more than strips of coloured fabric. They fell away, taking his hands, wrists, and forearms with them.

'*Clown…*'

Pierrot looked down at the heap of coloured material on the ground, a small wisp of smoke coming from it. Pierrot did not smile.

'That's better,' he said, turning back to the crowd. 'Back to normal.'

The last of the humans and their clowns were disappearing into the tent. Pierrot was ready to join them when he noticed, lurking behind one of the old caravans, something shining. Pierrot dropped the flap of his tent and peered through the gap, squinting at the twinkling, glimmering shapes in the distance.

He watched as they came closer, watched as they resolved into the forms of children.

No, not just children. The children. The boy, the girl, and her copy. The ones who had escaped. The ones who Harlequin had failed to track down. The ones who had come back to the circus, wearing mirrors.

Pierrot retreated to the darkness of his tent.

It would do no harm to let Harlequin have one last scene on centre stage.

Even if it was his death scene.

— CHAPTER THIRTY-ONE —

THE RING MASTER

'Welcome, greetings, and salutations to one and all!'

Harlequin stood in the centre of the Big Top, a single spotlight trained on him. It was a full house, humans and clowns all crammed in together, except for the two seats next to Albert and Tamara Wilson. Harlequin cast a suspicious eye across the crowd. No sign of the girl. No sign of the boy. No sign of the traitor Art. No sign of Pierrot. No matter; Harlequin would have his revenge on them all.

'I am Harlequin, your Ring Master, and tonight I have a most unusual show for you all.'

The crowd applauded rapturously.

'Bring it out!'

A small group of Dotores dragged the blue box, the box covered in stars, the famous Box of Mirrors, out into the middle of the Big Top. It was rickety and wobbling, sparks flying from the joints every time that it juddered over the ground. There was the smell of burning. The Dotore had done their best to put it back together again, but it was technology far beyond the brain of your average clown.

But the crowd ooh-ed and aah-ed either way.

'We've seen this box of tricks before, of course,' said Harlequin. 'And what a night that was, eh, my darlings? A night none of us will ever forget. A night that changed us all. You all took a little bit of the circus home that night with you, didn't you, my dears?'

Cheers from the crowd, some whooping. A 'Yes!' from somewhere near the back. Clapping.

'And now, the circus needs something back from you,' continued Harlequin. 'A little something, a simple favour, in compensation for all that we have given you.'

Outside, and out of sight, Hobo and the Lucys were listening.

'What's he doing?' asked Lucy.

'Putting on a show,' said Hobo. 'He wants them to do something for him.'

Lucy poked her head around the corner for a split second.

'He's got the box,' she said, ducking back.

'We should hang back,' said Hobo.

'My parents are going to wonder where we are,' said Wilson.

Lucy shot her an angry look. 'They're my parents.'

'They're my parents.'

Lucy rolled her eyes. 'Stop repeating!'

'I'm not!' said Wilson with a hiss. 'They *are* my parents. Just as much as they are yours.'

'We don't have time for this!' interrupted Hobo.

'Yes we do,' said Lucy. 'This is exactly why—'

'No,' said Hobo firmly. 'I mean it. We don't have time.'

He pointed down at Lucy's foot or, at least, at the space where Lucy's foot should have been. There was next to nothing there, just the ghostly outline of a trainer hovering over the grass.

'This was your plan, Lucy. Get you and Wilson back to the box. That's what you said. Well, we're here now and it looks like there's no going back.'

Inside, Harlequin was still in full flow.

'Come down to the front, Albert and Tamara!'

Albert and Tamara looked at each other dumbly. Without their clown to nudge them in the right direction, they weren't sure what to do.

'Give them a hand, ladies and gentlemen!' urged Harlequin. The people on either side of Albert and Tamara suddenly got to their feet and lunged at them, grabbing at their clothes and hauling them up out of their seats. The people in front turned around and pulled them forwards, dragging them out of their aisle and into the next. Hand over hand, person to person, Albert and Tamara were delivered down through the crowd. They offered no resistance, just stared dumbly at each other until finally they found themselves in a heap on the dusty floor of the Big Top. Some Dotores lifted them to their feet and manhandled them to a spot in front of Harlequin. Another spotlight flickered on, painting a weak circle of light onto them.

'Let's all take a look at Albert and Tamara,' said Harlequin, circling Lucy's parents like a shark circling two tired swimmers. 'Don't they look just wonderful together? The perfect couple.'

The crowd gave out an 'aahhh' in appreciation.

'But there's something missing!'

The crowd made a sad noise. One person, somewhere, boo-ed.

'What they really need, what would make their life just perfect is a little girl of their own, don't you think?'

The crowd cheered and clapped its agreement.

'We've got a little girl,' said Tamara quietly.

Harlequin hushed the crowd. 'What's that?' he said, feigning surprise. 'You've already got a little girl?'

'Yes,' said Tamara. Her voice was sluggish, like the voice of somebody woken from a dream they hadn't quite stopped dreaming yet.

'Well, if you already have a little girl,' said

Harlequin. 'Where on earth is she?'

A hush fell over the crowd. Tamara blinked a few times. Albert, unbidden, took her hand. Lucy's parents looked suddenly very alone, and very afraid.

'We don't know,' said Albert, slowly. 'She was with us and then— '

'She was with you?' said Harlequin. His pretence slipped for a second as he spun in circles, looking for Lucy. 'You mean she's here?'

'I… well…'

Albert and Tamara didn't get a chance to answer. Harlequin vaulted away from them and clambered nimbly up onto the top of the Box of Mirrors.

'Ladies and Gentlemen, I can tell just by looking at you that you are happy. You are at peace. And I can tell you that peace is a fragile thing. Peace can be shattered. Peace can be broken. Peace can be smashed up and ground under my boot until there is nothing left at all. Peace… by piece, by piece. Oh, I can tell you would like to keep your little town just the way it is now, just perfect and peaceful and well… I can tell you how to do that, if you like?'

As one, the crowd leaned forwards, both human and clown.

'I can tell you how to fix all your problems…'

Harlequin pointed down at Albert and Tamara, who were huddled together in the shadow of the Box of Mirrors, looking bewildered and afraid.

'Bring me their little girl. Bring me Lucy Wilson!'

The crowd rose as one from their seats – and froze.

'Spare yourself the bother, mate!'

The entire town fixed its eyes on Lucy Wilson.

'I'm already here!'

'And so am I!' The town blinked and cocked its head to the side as another Lucy Wilson stepped into view.

Harlequin clapped his hands together in glee.

'Oh my goodness!' he squealed. 'This is just too perfect. Now I get to put an end to you twice!'

'Don't think so.'

This voice came from the other side of the tent, opposite the entrance. As one, the town and Harlequin turned to look at the speaker. A spotlight flickered, its dirty yellow light illuminating a figure.

A small, hunched figure, holding a stick.

'Oh, you cannot be serious, you're dead!'

Punch and Judy Pete, Lord Punchinella, the last Prince of Punchinella, raised his head and grinned.

'You think that was end of Punchinella? No. Moment was prepared for.'

Before Harlequin could speak, tiny shadows appeared in the light around Punchinella's feet. With a click and a clack, small figures walked awkwardly forwards. Punchinella's puppets, twisted and dented and broken in places, limping, shuffling, but all seemingly alive.

'All of House Punchinella prepared.'

On the top of his broken down box, surrounded by his broken down clowns, Harlequin laughed.

'Ah, why not?' he cried. 'It's time for an encore!'

— CHAPTER THIRTY-TWO —

ENCORE

Hobo skidded to a halt between Lucy and Wilson. In the middle of the tent, Harlequin and Punchinella were fighting fiercely, Punchinella expertly ducking and weaving as Harlequin's blade carved through the air. Around them, the people of Ogmore fought a pitched battle with Punchinella's army of puppets. Kicking and flailing, the good people of Ogmore seemed to be losing against the onslaught of tiny, and surprisingly vicious, little wooden people.

'What exactly am I seeing?' asked Hobo. 'I'm afraid my brain just refuses to accept this.'

'Clowns,' said Lucy, very matter-of-factly. 'And puppets. I had a dream like this once.'

Hobo and Wilson both looked at Lucy sideways. 'What?'

'Doesn't matter, we still need a way to get back into that box. It feels like my leg has gone to sleep. Permanently. I'm afraid to look down there.'

Hobo and Wilson looked. Lucy's lower legs had

all but vanished, taking on the same strange and ghostly appearance as her feet.

'You're fine,' said Wilson.

Lucy laughed. 'You can't lie to yourself, Wilson. Mum told me that.'

'I remember,' Wilson replied.

Hobo looked at the two of them. The more insubstantial Lucy became, the more of a real person Wilson seemed. Bit by bit, Wilson was replacing Lucy, whether she wanted to or not.

'Right,' said Hobo, suddenly determined. 'Big crowd of mind-controlled folk who might quite like to stop us from doing what we want to do. Not the first time. Usual plan?'

'Head down and charge in, you mean?' replied Lucy.

'Yup,' said Hobo, dropping his head and taking a deep breath. 'Here we go!'

Together, the three of them ran towards the riotous crowd.

Incredibly, the puppets were still winning. Tangled in hair, hanging from ears and noses, dodging between stamping legs, they dragged people and clown alike down to the ground, where they swarmed on top of them, tying them up with the strings that hung loose from them. The people of Ogmore were fighting bravely, egged on by their insubstantial clown counterparts, but even the puppets that they managed to smash or stamp on simply gathered their pieces and literally pulled themselves back together again.

As the distance between them and the crowd grew smaller, Lucy and Wilson tucked in behind Hobo. His bulk was their battering ram. A clown turned and saw Hobo. Too late! It flung its arms up in terror as Hobo, his eyes closed tight, smashed into it. There was a popping noise, like a handful of balloons all bursting at once, and when Hobo opened his eyes the clown had vanished.

The crowd froze for a moment. Even Harlequin and Punchinella stopped fighting. Everyone listened to the quiet 'tap, tap, tap' of the clown trapped on the wrong side of the mirror strapped to Hobo's chest. Hobo allowed himself a grin as he looked back up at the stunned faces of the clowns in the crowd.

'Run?' he suggested.

The clowns all looked to Harlequin, his blade frozen in the air mid-thrust.

His nostrils flared with disgust.

'Cowards,' he snorted.

The clowns all began to run, quickly followed by any human not already tied up. Mr and Mrs Wilson were the last to leave. They looked at Lucy and Wilson, blinking and turning their heads from side to side as if they were seeing double – which, of course, they sort of were.

'Go home,' said Lucy. 'This is just a dream.'

Mr Wilson tugged at Mrs Wilson's arm and, walking slowly backwards, they left the Big Top. Lucy and Wilson did their best to ignore them. Whatever happened next, it was best that they weren't here.

'Follow them,' said Punchinella gruffly to his puppets, nodding at the retreating crowd. 'Keep all safe.'

A puppet, in what might have been a military uniform, gave a stiff salute and led the other puppets, hopping, crawling and limping behind him, out of the tent.

An awkward silence descended.

'Well, that was easy,' said Wilson.

'You think they'll believe it was a dream?' asked Hobo.

'Yeah, of course,' said Lucy. 'Who hasn't had the clown and puppet dream, right?'

Hobo and Wilson didn't get the chance to answer.

'I rather think you're forgetting someone,' said Harlequin. He was leaning languidly against the Box of Mirrors, his knife in his hand. He twirled it back and forth, his eyes fascinated by the patterns that it left in the air as it cut through the fabric of the world.

'No,' replied Punchinella. 'You forget. You forget I teach you, long ago, to fight. You forget I know you. And you still forget to keep guard up.'

'What do you—' said Harlequin. 'Oh!' He reached down and patted his side. A flap of fabric fell away, revealing a deep scarlet wound. 'Oh, well done, old boy,' he said. His legs suddenly fell from under him, and he crumpled into a heap on the floor.

Punchinella kicked Harlequin's blade away across the dirt floor of the Big Top, and knelt down beside him.

'You're not going to crowd my death scene, are you?' said Harlequin, coughing.

Punchinella took Harlequin's hand in his. 'No,' he said softly, 'you are star.'

'I am rather, aren't I?'

Harlequin reached up to his chest with the free hand not clasping his wound.

'Take a look,' he said, 'underneath.'

Punchinella gently peeled open the skin-tight patchwork suit that covered Harlequin's body. Underneath there was another, simpler garment, with the same colours and coat of arms as Punchinella's.

'You kept house,' said Punchinella choking slightly on the words.

'Next to my heart,' replied Harlequin. 'Always.'

'Home,' said Punchinella. 'You come home now.'

'I blew home up, don't you… remember?'

'Home is not place,' replied Punchinella, taking Harlequin's hand and placing it on his own chest.

'Come home,' he said again.

But Harlequin could not answer. Harlequin was dead.

And that, perhaps, should have been an end to it. It was certainly how Harlequin would have liked things to have ended, with a close up of him, then the screen slowly fading to black, an unseen orchestra striking up, and not a dry eye in the house. Life, however, was not a story and did not stick to such lines.

In life, there is often loose ends.

'Congratulations,' Pierrot called out, strolling into the tent calmly. 'Well done, one and all. But I'm afraid you won't be winning the day. Allow me to introduce myself. My name is—'

'Pierrot,' interrupted Punchinella, his voice full of fury.

'Indeed and—'

But Pierrot wasn't going to get centre stage either. Not in this moment.

Centre stage instead went to the sound of breaking glass as two mirrors fell to the floor.

Centre stage went to Lucy, and her amazing disappearing trick.

But sadly she wasn't there to enjoy it.

Lucy was gone.

— CHAPTER THIRTY-THREE —

MAN IN THE MIRROR

Lucy woke up staring at herself in the mirror. She rolled over, and there she was again. Above, below, behind, everywhere she looked – there she was.

'Urgh,' she said groggily. 'I'm in that box again.'

'Me too,' said one of the other Lucys.

Lucy sat up and let her eyes focus properly. All the other Lucys did the same, except for one.

'All right, Wilson?' asked Lucy.

'All right,' said Wilson.

The two girls, or one girl in two halves depending on your point of view, sat and stared at the mirrors for a while. Something was wrong, and it was only a few moments before Wilson realised what it was.

'I don't have a reflection,' she said, her voice cracking slightly.

Lucy had noticed it too, but she hadn't had the heart to say anything. The more time she spent with Wilson, the more real she seemed. Lucy had even wondered if she, not Wilson, might be the copy. But here, in the place where it had all really started, there could be no doubt.

Lucy choked back a sob as tears began to roll down Wilson's face.

'I don't have a reflection,' said Wilson again, her voice full of anguish.

Lucy reached out for her doppelganger, turning her around by the shoulders so that they were facing each other.

'Of course you do,' said Lucy gently. 'I'm right here.'

The two Lucy's embraced each other and nobody, not even they could have told you which one moved first or how long they sat there, each holding the other, crying as one.

However long it was, it only ended when a sound began to reverberate around the box. The sound of footsteps.

Lucy broke away from Wilson, quickly drying her eyes on her sleeve. Whoever was coming, whatever creature or clown or alien from the other side of space, she was Lucy Lethbridge-Stewart-Wilson, and she would meet them face to face and on her feet.

The footsteps grew closer. Lucy turned around and around, searching each of the mirrors for the source of the sound. Wilson got shakily to her feet as well, drying her eyes as Lucy had. Her hand found Lucy's and the two girls began to circle as one.

'Where's it coming from?' whispered Wilson.

'The mirror,' said Lucy.

'Which one?'

A gentle tap on glass gave the answer. The two girls spun instantly to face the noise behind them.

There, stepping carefully through the glass was a man wearing a British Military uniform.

'I'd say good morning or good afternoon,' he said, his voice kind and stern at the same time. 'I'm afraid I don't have the time... '

'Grandad?' said Lucy with a gasp.

The man in the uniform looked at her curiously and twitched his moustache

Lucy stared back. It had to be him. Younger yes, wiry and strong in a way that she had never known him to be, but still the same man. The same eyes. The same voice. Of course, Lucy knew that you could have said the same about her and Wilson, but she knew that this was different. The same eyes, the same voice, and the same feeling in Lucy's heart when she looked at him.

'What's your name, young lady?' he asked

'Lucy...'

The man raised an eyebrow.

'Lucy who, might I ask?'

Lucy winced. Wilson squeezed her hand. 'It's OK. Tell him.'

'I'm Lucy Wilson,' said Lucy. 'But you can call me Lucy Lethbridge-Stewart.'

The man smiled and extended his hand towards her.

'Brigadier Alistair Lethbridge-Stewart,' he said formally. 'I believe we've already met, although for me this is rather the first time and quite unexpected.'

Lucy grasped her grandad's hand and shook it earnestly.

'You believe me?' she asked.

'Of course I believe you,' replied Grandad. 'Obviously, clearly a Lethbridge-Stewart. You've got the look.'

'We don't really look alike...' said Lucy, trying not to sound too rude. Things were different in the time this version of her grandad came from, after all.

Her grandad scoffed. 'In the eyes, girl, in the eyes!' he said, his voice firm but still kind. 'We all get it, once we've seen things. And you've seen things, haven't you?'

They looked into the mirror together, the girl and the man who would one day be her grandfather. Lucy had to admit, it was there, in the eyes.

'How about me?' asked Wilson keenly, popping up behind Lucy.

Lucy had almost forgotten about her doppelganger for a moment. Being here, being with her grandad, all the alien boxes and creepy clowns and mysterious doubles in the universe couldn't have spoilt that. There was so much she wanted to ask him, so much she wanted to say. She didn't know which of the million different thoughts would spill out of her mouth first, but she opened it to speak all the same.

'Now, down to business,' interrupted Grandad and, without warning, he pulled the two girls towards them and embraced them.

He felt a little different than Lucy remembered. Firmer and stronger, no doubt because he was younger, but everything else was the same. It felt right. It felt like it had always felt before and, for a moment, every second that Lucy had ever spent with her grandad flashed before her eyes. It was joyous, and surprising, filled with both precious memories that she already cherished and wonderful moments long forgotten. It felt like forever, but moved by so fast and Lucy couldn't but catch her breath as the pictures and sounds and feelings began to change and she knew that she was coming towards the end. Towards his end.

Grandad let go. He turned away for a moment and although Lucy could have seen his face in the mirror if she'd wanted to, she turned away and looked at her own reflection in the mirror instead. And although she should probably have felt sad, or sorrowful, or lost, or afraid, all she did was smile.

The box hadn't just given her these moments with a younger version of her grandfather, it had given her all the moments she'd already had all over again. Living them again, she'd seen so much more and felt so much more.

She felt complete.

And complete was what she was. There was no more Lucy and Wilson. There was just Lucy, and Lucy Wilson, and Lucy Lethbridge-Stewart, and they were all one and the same – the mixed race girl with the unmanageable hair, cocky smile, and 'the look' in her eyes.

'Well, that worked then,' said Grandad, seemingly back to his normal self. 'I must say, considering I've only existed for a few seconds I'm making a rather good job of this.'

'A few seconds?' asked Lucy.

Grandad gave her an embarrassed, very un-Lethbridge-Stewart like smile. 'Yes, I rather think so, I'm afraid. The ring you have there?'

Lucy looked down the ring.

'What about it?'

'It's rather more than it appears. It's been helping you, you know.'

'I know.'

'It's still helping you...'

Grandad waited a moment for Lucy to catch on.

'*You're*... the ring?' said Lucy.

204

'Yes. No. In a manner of speaking. The ring and the box come from the same place, you see. A place where things aren't always what they seem. It's good at hiding, of making itself look like something you understand.'

'I thought you were him,' said Lucy, her voice tinged with anguish.

'And in every way that matters, I am. I'm the part of him that you carry with you, Lucy. You remember your grandfather at the end of his life, but you remember him like this to. You remember his stories, his great adventures. They are a part of you, just like that other Lucy was. I may be gone right now but, I'm far from forgotten, aren't I?'

Lucy gave a sad smile. 'There, but not there?'

Grandad smiled back, then gave a stiff salute.

'Ready for duty.'

Lucy took a deep breath and composed herself. There was a part of her that wanted to stay here forever, but that wasn't the Lethbridge-Stewart way. It's wasn't Lucy's way

'I have to get back,' said Lucy reluctantly. 'I'm not sure I want to but... I have to. It's...'

'It's what we do,' said Grandad, finishing Lucy's sentence for her. 'It's our duty.' In a flash he pulled his revolver from the holster strapped to his hip and levelled the gun at a point past Lucy's head.

'I'd get down and cover your ears if I were you.'

Lucy didn't need to be told twice. She dropped to the floor, clasped her hands firmly over her ears and screwed her eyes shut tight. The shot sounded like thunder, with the sound reflecting and rebounding back and forth

Lucy opened her eyes. The mirror was still there, still gleaming, still reflecting the image of Lucy and her not-yet-but-one-day-grandfather back at the two of them. Except, there was one tiny difference. A crack, no bigger than a penny, a little above Lucy's reflection's head.

'Do you, err, have any more bullets?' asked Lucy sheepishly.

Grandad gave Lucy a wry look. 'I usually only need the one...'

And, as they watched, the crack the size of a penny began to slowly get larger. With a creak, the crack became two cracks, then three, then four, then a myriad more. The cracks began to spread like the threads of a spider's web, tracing their way across the glass and hoping from mirror the mirror. Their reflections, Lucy's and Grandad's, became fractured and distorted as the mirror world around them began to break down.

'This is starting to look like a bad idea,' said Lucy.

'I would be so sure about that,' said Grandad, pointing to a spot in the wall where the mirrors had begun to fall away.

There, behind where the mirror had been, where by rights there should have been wood or maybe plaster, was the Earth. Small, blue-green, roundish, and hurtling through space.

Lucy watched as the little ball of blue and green grew closer, as the smudges of colour turned into continents, then countries, then came close enough that patches of brown and grey began to take over the green, and the cities of the world became visible one by one.

'Looks like we're coming down somewhere over Wales,' said Grandad, peering through the gap. 'Lovely part of the world, actually.'

More glass fell away as the world rushed towards them, or they fell towards it – either way it started to fall faster and faster, exploding into powder as it hit the floor.

'Coming down?' asked Lucy, raising her voice over the howling sound of the box hitting Earth's atmosphere.

— CHAPTER THIRTY-FOUR —
GIRL WITH TWO FACES

Pierrot had been just about to say something devastatingly witty when the box exploded, blowing him off his feet. At least, that's what he told people afterwards. The truth was that he was chased around the box by an old puppeteer and a boy wearing mirrors stolen from a girls' toilet. Somehow, though, that made for less of a story.

The box *did* explode – that bit was true.

Pierrot picked himself up gingerly. Punchinella and the boy did the same. The old man was remarkably spry for his age, but the boy was a mess of cuts and bruises from the broken glass of his mirror armour.

'Boy OK?' asked Punchinella.

'Boy OK,' said Hobo with a wince. 'Well, sort of.'

Pierrot stepped towards them.

'You will both stop this nonsense,' he said, his voice haughty and proud. 'I am Lord Pierrot, of

House Pierrot, of the Great Court of Clown. I am consort to the beauty Columbine, and this world is owed to me by the ancient laws of our people.'

Punchinella spat on the floor at Pierrot's feet.

Hobo flexed, ready to take another charge, but before he could do anything, another voice rang out, just as clear and strong as Pierrot's, but far more welcome.

'No.'

Pierrot turned, slowly.

Lucy was standing, calm and alone, in the middle of the Big Top.

'Lucy!' shouted Hobo.

'In the flesh,' she replied with a smile. 'All of it.'

'Wilson?'

'That's me.'

'Lethbridge Stewart?'

'Lethbridge-Stewart?' said Pierrot, his voice trembling slightly. He looked from Lucy to Punchinella, from Punchinella to Hobo, from Hobo back to Lucy. Punchinella's puppets had formed themselves into neat ranks at the old man's feet, smacking their tiny fists into their wooden palms in menacing unison.

Lucy took a step towards the black and white clown.

'My name,' she said calmly, 'is Lucy Wilson. Some people call me Lucy Lethbridge-Stewart. You know that name, don't you?'

Pierrot shook his head. 'It is an old story, nothing more.'

'Nothing more?' said Lucy mockingly. 'But you are clown. Stories mean something to you, don't they?'

Behind Pierrot, Punchinella laughed darkly. 'Girl understands,' he said, chuckling to himself.

'And what's more,' continued Lucy, 'I think you know my story. I think you know about me, and my family, and what we are. I think you know that this world is protected, and has been protected, by us for a good while now. That's why invasions start here, in Ogmore. You're not looking for a sleepy little town where nobody will notice you sneaking around. You're banging on the front door. Wherever I am, it's always going to be the same, isn't it? Aliens. Monsters. You come here because if you can get past me, well... you think taking the rest of Earth will be easy.'

Lucy strode towards Pierrot. The clown didn't move. They stared at each other, girl and alien, neither one ready to blink or give an inch.

'I am Lucy Lethbridge-Stewart, Defender of Earth.'

'I am Pierrot, Lord of —'

'Do you know what a pantomime is?' interrupted Lucy.

The clown looked at her confused.

'You know,' Lucy carried on. 'Middle-aged men dressed up as middle-aged ladies, lots of thigh slapping, probably a dodgy song and dance number?'

'Ha! Cheap human entertainment,' said Pierrot with a laugh. 'I am clown. I show you the true pantomime.'

'Will it still have my favourite bit?'

Pierrot leaned forwards, so close that Lucy could feel the cold paint on the tip on his nose brushing against her own.

'And what, child, might that be?'

Lucy grinned. 'You must know it. It's totally the best bit. So, the bad guy, he's looking in one direction and someone's distracting him, the audience all know but he doesn't, and all the while...'

Pierrot's eyes snapped wide in sudden realisation.

'He's behind you!' said Lucy.

Hobo brought the mirror from Ogmore Secondary School's girls' toilets crashing down on Pierrot's head. There was a strange sound as it made contact, a mix of glass shattering and air rushing into a freshly created, clown-shaped vacuum.

Shards of glass fell like snowflakes, a flurry of light and reflections. The circus, in miniature, splintered into the air, Pierrot the clown trapped within.

Hobo dropped the shattered frame of the mirror to the ground then threw his arms around Lucy, hugging her so tightly that he almost squeezed the air out of her lungs.

'You're… crushing…' gasped Lucy.

Hobo let go, a huge smile across his face. 'You're back,' he said happily.

'I'm back,' confirmed Lucy.

'Where did you go?'

'I had things to do,' said Lucy. 'You know… Lethbridge-Stewart stuff.'

She looked past Hobo at the smoking ruins of the big blue box. Hobo followed her gaze and, without either of them saying a word, Hobo knew that whatever had happened in there would stay just there. It was another part of Lucy's world that he wasn't allowed admittance to, but this time he didn't mind. It didn't feel like a secret. Whatever it was, it felt like a gift – one that was for Lucy alone.

Punchinella shuffled up beside them.

'Is nice,' he said. 'Girl, boy, back together. But probably want to run now.'

'Run?' asked Lucy.

'Run,' said Punchinella. His eyes fell to the floor, and to the glass strewn across it. The glass was… moving.

Lucy and Hobo looked at each other.

'Run!'

CHAPTER THIRTY-FIVE

ANOTHER RUBBISH MONSTER

Lucy and Hobo ran through the Big Top. Behind them something crunched and screeched itself into life with a sound like a thousand fingernails scraping down a blackboard made out of nightmares.

'Should have known that was too easy,' said Hobo with a gasp.

Lucy glanced back over her shoulder as the pieces of glass from the mirror billowed up like a tiny tornado. In every shard was a tiny Pierrot, a pale angry face screaming silently on the other side of the glass. The tornado began to gather the debris of the big blue box.

'We can handle it!' Lucy shouted to Hobo over the noise.

'How?' asked Hobo. 'We're a bit far from the swimming pool.'

'I'll think of something,' replied Lucy. They burst

out of the tent and into the cold night air. It was a cloudy night, and above the circus there wasn't a single star in the sky.

'Lights,' she said.

'What?' asked Hobo.

'We need to turn out the lights.'

The thing burst out of the Big Top – twelve feet or more of broken glass, wood, dirt, and whatever else it had been able to grab hold of as it cobbled itself together. Lucy could see some of Punchinella's puppets, frantically trying to escape, like tiny swimmers being dragged out to sea. Except that, in this case, the sea had arms, and legs, and a face. A face that was looking right down at Lucy.

'You will not beat me!' said the thing, a hundred tiny Pierrots all screaming at once.

Lucy stood her ground, staring defiantly back up at the monster. The lights of the circus danced: reds and yellows and greens.

'I already beat you,' she said, her voice calm and strong. 'Now, it's time for you to go.'

'I am Lord Pierrot, of House Pierrot.'

'Heard it!' shouted Lucy, holding her hand up to the monster. 'We already did that bit.'

The creature's face split open, jagged pieces of glass arranging themselves into razor sharp teeth.

'Then maybe I'll skip to the bit where I eat you, little girl.'

Lucy raised an eyebrow. 'Eat me? Really? You're going to eat me?'

In the corner of her eye Lucy saw Hobo waving. He'd tracked down the generator. Lucy swallowed. She was pretty sure that this would work. But her plan relied on two assumptions – firstly that the mysterious alien circus still used conventional electricity, and secondly that Hobo could pull the main power lead out of the rather shoddy-looking generator without electrocuting himself.

All in all, it wasn't the worst plan Lucy had ever put into action.

The sparkling, technicolor face of the creature bent slowly down towards Lucy, its body creaking and scraping and crunching against itself. It was so close that Lucy could see herself reflected back, her face mixing with Pierrot's, the lights of the circus dancing through both of them. Cold, alien rage burned in the clown's eyes.

'It's time, little girl.'

Lucy smiled. 'You're right. Show's over.'

Right on cue, Hobo yanked the main power cable out of the generator. There was a small burst of sparks and then, after a momentary flicker, all of the lights went out. The mirrored glass went dark and, as it did so, Lucy's reflection began to disappear. And so did Pierrot's.

The creature crumbled, only glass, wood and

rubbish once more, sending up a cloud of dust as it hit the ground. Lucy watched as Punchinella's puppets pulled themselves free of the wreckage, aided by their comrades.

Hobo trotted over.

'How did you know that would work?' he asked.

'I've spent a lot of time looking in mirrors lately,' replied Lucy, 'And besides... it was a rubbish monster.'

THE CIRCUS LEAVES TOWN

Things went back to normal fairly quickly after that, the same old comfortable and reliable normal that Ogmore had always known before Lucy turned up.

Albert and Tamara Wilson went back to their day-to-day routine, although Albert seemed to be working from home a lot more, and they both swore off coffee for good. Hobo returned to being the school oddball instead of its academic superstar. Crime, disorder, and anti-social behaviour bounced back to normal Ogmore levels (which meant barely noticeable in Lucy's book). Not to mention everyone went about their lives without the guidance of invisible clowns.

Lucy and Hobo could hang out for a while with friends who knew nothing about anything Lethbridge-Stewart-shaped, or all the dangers that came with it. Maya was serene as always, as if there was nothing bad in the world that couldn't be changed when she became a barrister; Paula was working on a brand new cookie recipe for that world. No one, even Hobo's friend, Will, who still got angry about most things, seemed to remember anything dodgy about clowns. One more secret to carry around for Lucy Wilson and Hobo Kostinen, and something else she couldn't tell Ayesha when they had their regular catch-up.

The circus was still on the edge of town, although nobody seemed to notice it except Lucy and Hobo. Even Hobo forgot it was there sometimes. Some lingering after-effect of the clowns' influence made sure that nobody ventured in its direction. Slowly, piece by piece, the circus collapsed in on itself. Lucy had nicknamed the abandoned circus 'Little Porthcawl', much to Hobo's annoyance.

While everyone else was getting back to normal, Lucy still felt anything but.

But people who don't fit in have a knack for finding each other, and it was this knack that one rainy Saturday morning led Lucy to Punchinella (although he preferred to be called Pete). He was standing on the grass verge watching the circus slowly disappear. Mum had sent Lucy down to the shops for tea bags (which were now very important in the coffee-free Wilson household), and in true

Lucy fashion, she was taking as long as possible about it.

Lucy took a spot next to Pete, and they stood for a moment in silence, just watching the circus.

'Girl confused, I expect,' said Pete, breaking the silence.

'Not really,' Lucy replied. 'Just a bit…'

'Confused.'

'OK, yeah.'

Pete reached into the pocket of his cardigan and pulled out a small ball of thread.

'Take,' he said, offering the thread to Lucy.

'What is it?'

'Is line,' replied Pete. 'Like… family line. Blood line. Join us together.'

'Me and you?'

'Everyone.'

'Now I *am* confused,' said Lucy.

'You see something in box,' said Pete. 'I know.'

Lucy shuffled her feet. 'It was my grandfather,' she said. 'But not like he was when I knew him, before he died. He was younger.'

'Is the line,' said Pete matter-of-factly. 'Family line. Blood line.'

Lucy stared at her ring. 'Actually I think it was something else.' She shuffled her feet again, not sure what else to say. It was then that she realised that there were two suitcases on the ground at Pete's feet.

'Going somewhere?' she asked. 'You know the bus doesn't come down here, right?'

Pete smiled. 'I am clown. Clown not take bus. Look!'

He pointed across the road to the circus. Lucy peered at where his finger was pointing and, past the hedge and the outer tents, barely visible inside the Big Top, she could see tiny figures moving. Tiny figures moving and climbing. Climbing on something blue.

'The box!' gasped Lucy. 'I thought it was gone. Can I…?'

'Girl cannot go back in box,' he said. His voice was sad, but firm. 'Circus closed to girl forever.'

'Where are you going?' asked Lucy.

'In box,' said Pete. 'I find something now.'

Lucy watched as Pete headed towards the circus. The place seemed to breathe a sigh of relief as he entered, and its slow, agonising collapse seemed to grow a little faster, as if the whole place had been holding its breath until that moment. She watched as the flap of the tent closed behind him.

Lucy waited for a moment or two, but she knew, in the strange way that she knew a lot of things, that she would never see the strange old Punch and Judy man again.

She looked down at the little ball of thread in her hand.

'Time line,' she said. She wasn't sure if it made any sense to her, but somehow holding onto that little ball of thread made her feel… peaceful. Whole. She could be Lucy Wilson and Lucy Lethbridge-Stewart. Ogmore could be the alien weirdness capital of the world.

And while she worked all those things out, her mum really wanted those tea bags.

About the Author

Chris Lynch is a writer, technologist and hypnotist living and working in Cardiff.

Chris has written for a wide range of publications in the UK and the US including *The Judge Dredd Megazine, Arcana, Metaverse, The Psychedelic Journal of Time Travel, 2026 Books, Accent UK, Something Wicked, The Sorrow, The Mad Scientist Journal, KZine, Wilde Times, Another Realm, 10thology, Midnight Hour* and *Insomnia Publications.*

Chris is also the author of *The Budget Android Tablet Buyer's Guide*, an Amazon #1 best-seller in the *Android Tablets* book category. Chris specialises in creating eBooks and online articles that help users make better IT decisions.

In 2015 Chris wrote the short feature *The Black Room* which is now available to watch on Amazon Prime and You Tube.

This is his first book for young people.

The Lucy Wilson Mysteries: Avatars of the Intelligence by Sue Hampton

Lucy Wilson doesn't want to move from London to sleepy South Wales. But when she arrives at her new seaside home, it doesn't appear to be as boring as she expected.

Ogmore-by-Sea seems to be under the control of a mysterious and powerful force. But why is Lucy its target? And why, when students at her new school start to disappear, does no one seem to care?

With the help of her new friend Hobo, Lucy Wilson must assume the mantle of her grandfather, the legendary Brigadier Lethbridge-Stewart, and defeat an invisible enemy before it's too late.

ISBN: 978-0-9957436-9-4

The Norris Girls by Nigel Hinton

Dad is away in a dangerous place, but life must go on for the Norris girls.

Beth dreams of being in the school musical, especially when super cool Josh gets the lead part.

Georgy trains every day, trying to win a place in the Inter-Counties Athletics Championships but first she has to beat her arch-rival, Layla.

And Katie wants an animal to look after – a dog or a cat or a rabbit would do, but if she could choose one thing in the whole world it would be a pony.

Filled with tears and laughter, heartache and longing, this is Little Women for the twenty-first century.

ISBN: 978-0-9955595-1-6

Also available from Candy Jar Books

The House on March Lane by Michelle Briscombe

In 1836, Harriet's papa, a ship's officer on HMS Beagle, returns from a long journey at sea. On his arrival home, Harriet and her friend Lily become involved in a dangerous secret with tragic consequences.

Almost two centuries later, Flora's best friend Archie experiences a ghostly encounter at her dad's reclamation and salvage yard.

The haunting takes the two friends on a detective adventure with a difference, and leads them to an unexpected and supernatural discovery.

Flora and Archie & Harriet and Lily's lives are soon entwined in a way that they could never have imagined possible.

ISBN: 978-0-9933221-2-9

Also available from Candy Jar Books

Will's War by Cherry Cobb

Will is an ordinary boy who likes to build Lego models and play with his dog, Rollo. But after a stupid row with his mum, he ends up at his grandad's house, where he discovers an old air raid shelter.

Will steps inside to investigate, but when he comes out he is not in his grandad's garden, but in Second World War London.

How will he get back?

ISBN: 978-0-9957436-8-7

The Crumble Lady by Lorraine Bowen

The Crumble Lady is a SUBURBAN SUPERHERO!

When she's not busy solving crimes, she's making cat food crumble, writing songs, and even getting her chums to save her town from a SHERBET EXPLOSION!

There's NEVER a dull moment with the Crumble Lady!

Tuck into a delicious portion of stories, funny characters and, of course, crumbles!

Lorraine Bowen shot to fame on *Britain's Got Talent* by winning David Walliams' Golden Buzzer for her jolly Crumble Song.

Featuring five scrumalicious crumble recipes!

ISBN: 978-0-99574336-7-0

Also available from Candy Jar Books

The Book Spy by Mark Carton

The Book Spy tells the remarkable story of arguably the greatest spy network of all time. This is not MI5 or the CIA, but a network of children focused on discovering the most important stories from around the globe, and getting them back to the UK.

From the early 1940s at Bletchley Park to modern day South Wales, The Book Spy highlights the crucial work done by operatives of the Children's Reading Intelligence Agency (CRIA), which was formed in the early 1940s by penpals who communicated secretly during the war.

ISBN: 978-0-9957436-6-3